The Elotes Man Will Soon Be Gone

Written by the students of
John Marshall High School

In conjunction with

 826LA

John Marshall High School Student Editorial Board
Rebecca Bowden, Margareth Lobo, Melanie Perez

The Elotes Man Will Soon Be Gone

Published November 2007 by 826LA

ISBN 978-0-9790073-3-0

First Edition

826LA
SPARC Building
685 Venice Boulevard
Venice, CA 90291
310.305.8418
www.826la.org

Book Design/Cover: Travis Schooley

Printed in Canada by WestCan P.G.

Distributed by PGW

CONTENTS

John Marshall High School Student Editorial Board:
Rebecca Bowden, Margareth Lobo, and Melanie Perez

INTRODUCTION

The noble, benevolent elotes man proudly parades the streets of Los Angeles, graciously providing mayonnaise-covered steamed corn to famished LA pedestrians. Every day, he arms himself with his most powerful weapons of tastiness (mayonnaise, mustard, butter, parmesan cheese, chili, and—of course—corn) as he fortuitously ventures out into the battlefield of food vending.

Unfortunately, like every great ear of corn in history, the elotes man will soon be gone. And with him, the world around him—our Los Angeles, the real Los Angeles written about in our stories and essays—will fade. The only way that the essence of this great corn-selling warrior can be saved is through the written word. By capturing this moment in time, we are creating immortality.

Most people don't know the city in the way that we do. TV depicts high schools as if they are always in suburban communities, where everyone knows everyone. Many people believe that John Marshall, a school featured in many TV shows and movies, is just another TV high school. Wrong! Marshall is nothing like the TV portrayals; it's more like a city itself. With more than 4,000 students on its beautiful campus, it's always busy and filled with more R-rated drama than a movie can handle. It is a marvelous place with so many people who are having problems worse than—like Oh My GOD!—a bad hair day.

Many people come to Los Angeles for the weather, Hollywood, and the hipster lifestyle. But they don't realize what the people who have lived here all their lives do: just because Hollywood lies within LA doesn't mean that it's the only great thing to come and see. Hollywood contributes much to John Marshall's history, but Marshall is more than that. We students know who we are, even though Hollywood does not. The mix of people within Marshall is so vast that it's a surprise that not one of our stories is told by Hollywood. Then again, we didn't know we would tell these stories either.

When our teacher, Ms. Patterson, asked us to write a "personal essay," many of us were unsure of what to write about. When we handed in our first rough drafts, she realized we hadn't really thought about it. She had a little talk with each of us, and afterwards we all had a better idea of what we were supposed to do. And later, after we met the encouraging 826LA editors and heard their compliments, we put in more effort and more time to draft and redraft. We even started to act like writers—we changed our minds over sentences, and threw out entire paragraphs and rewrote them.

By the end of the process, some of us had written about deaths or young love. Others wrote about moving to the United States or just walking through different neighborhoods, where the ice cream man or elotes man might dwell. And though he will soon be gone, like hip social scenes and Hollywood trends, our writing—about the real Los Angeles—will still be here.

On behalf of all of the authors, we would like to thank Julius Diaz Panoriñgan at 826LA for dealing with our disturbing conversations during editorial board meetings, as well as all of the 826LA tutors and editors. Special thanks go to Travis Schooley, this book's designer, and Heidi Pickman, who coordinated radio production for our essays. We would also like to thank our principal, Daniel Harrison; our teachers—David Dandridge, Paul Payne, Teri Klass, and Eric Womack—who allowed us to work on this project during class time; and most importantly, our teacher, Jane Patterson, for every last drop of support. Lastly, we would like to thank Teresa Bourgoise for bringing 826LA and John Marshall High School together.

Nicolei Buendia

TOGETHER THROUGH THE DISTANCE

He and I walk in harmony under the pouring rain. His glasses are covered with swollen rain drops. I offer my assistance; he hands me his glasses, and I rub the lenses on a dry portion of my jacket, yet this only blurs his vision when he puts them back on. My jacket is almost entirely soaked. All our clothes are too, though I am calm in the presence of rain. The rain has a refreshing aroma as if initiating a renewal.

He is beside me here, walking at my pace, or I am at his. He removes his glasses; a thick black frame borders lenses of almost the same width. The lenses are fogged and smudged. He thinks my attempt to wipe them clear is amusing, and he laughs.

"At least you tried," he says.

I notice the imprints of our shoes behind us as we walk toward our destinations. Our conversations extend like our steps, always in motion. He wears a khaki sweater unzipped, showing his plain blue t-shirt over a black one, yet they are a shade darker from the moisture. He appears as if he swam with his clothes on. His hair is clustered at different angles yet mostly flattened by the weight of rain.

I ask, "Are your parents going to be mad if you come home wet?"

His face is low. "It's not parents—it's just my mom. Don't worry; she won't get mad."

He gives me a comfortable smile; his cheeks rise, and the lines around his smile become well-defined. I grip the strap of my bag, tight on its coarse edges. I am cut off from breathing. Recollections pierce through my chest as my mind traces back to when I lost my father. I recall feeling empty and incomplete. I had distrusted those who retold my past and yearned to see the truth for myself.

He too has a mother and no father. I am no longer alone. I no longer feel incomplete. We know little of each other, yet it does not seem so. We are like two hands fitting into each other perfectly. He guides my feet as my mind drifts away. The rain is loud around us; I can only hear our voices.

We speak endlessly in conversations that are often silly. I feel the world is distant. "My eyes are black," I say. We are able to talk about anything, to the point where one topic springs into other topics so often it is impossible to figure out how one began.

He says, "That's impossible! No one has black eyes."

"Look!" I signal to him. I stand in front of him and bring my head up slightly to align my eyes with his. I cast myself into his eyes and marvel at their luminescence. His skin is smooth and creamed-mocha in color. I feel his slow, light breaths on my skin.

His eyes are fixed onto mine. He squints his eyes then widens them. He pauses for a moment, and abruptly he concludes, "See, they're not black. They're brown!"

"My student ID says black, but some say dark brown. I think they turn brown in the sun." Do eyes change color?

The rain lessens to sprinkling. My feet are cold. The pavement is damp and dark. We have arrived at the corner. He waits with me for the light to switch. Green. I place one foot ahead. He embraces me, and I nearly lose my balance. Although the rain is cold on my skin, he provides my body with warmth and comfort. He captivates me although he does not know it. He told me once before that he hugs all his friends as a way to say good-bye, but it is a little suspicious of him to say. I can't figure out a way to react. I smile and say, "Bye."

Winter is near ending and we walk together. The sky is a bright, radiant white. He steps onto a large stone that serves as a border between the paved road behind us and the downhill sands ahead. The long trails of cracks make me feel unstable. I am frightened by the altitude. I tell him, "If you fall, I'm gonna kick you."

He laughs and asks, "So you would kick me while I'm already dead?"

Even though I am embarrassed, I laugh too. "Yeah." Why did I say that in the first place? Stupid.

"Come." He presents his hand to me, and I allow him to take mine. I step onto the stone as I grip his hand firmly.

Beyond the mountain, the city is beautiful. The buildings present a promising landscape of security and trust. I am awed by the peaceful sight of the city. He braces his arms over my shoulders and around me, and he holds me close. I ask, "Does this mean we're going out?"

"Didn't I already tell you?"

"Yeah, but we didn't really say it." Putting love into words is complex. Two birds simply know what it is when they feel it.

"OK then. Nicolei," he started, "will you go out with me?"

"OK." We smile at one another.

Bianca Huezo

LADIES, WHO DO WE LOVE?

Every time I hear about relationships, I know there is a girl out there who was hurt by a guy, her "man." I was one of those girls who loved to love and be loved back. Most girls choose someone who they think will protect them. They choose someone who is important at school—someone who is cute, tough, sweet, bad, and troubled—someone who says, "I love you, Baby." Ladies, who do we love? The ones who are sweet or the ones who hurt us? I wonder why I pick one and not the other.

I met "Angel" at school. When I was with my friends, he came up to me with an innocent face and a bright smile that showed two dimples and made him shine. I knew right away that he was special. Angel was fourteen, smart, athletic, charming, and honest. I wasn't in love with him at first because I didn't know him, but I talked to him as if I knew him already. I shared things with him, and I wasn't embarrassed. He would never tell me anything that would make me mad, sad, or disappointed. This, I think, was the first step in his mission to get me to start liking him. As time went by, he tried and tried and tried to complete that mission—and then he succeeded.

Love is something beautiful, something you like feeling when it's there. When I was dating Angel, I was in paradise, as if the world was just me and him. I didn't think that anybody would make me feel the way he did. Every morning on my way to school, I couldn't wait to see him, and I became so happy once I did. His letters let me know how much he loved me and how lucky he felt to have me. Yes, I fell for it; every girl does. As my love grew bigger every day, I knew that the bond wouldn't break, that it couldn't break. Later, I tried strongly to keep that bond tied together,

3

but it wasn't tight enough.

My dad never agreed with what people would tell him. *"Deje que su hija sea feliz, habrá un día en que ella se casara ¿y qué haría usted?"* they would say. (Let your daughter be happy; there will be one day when she will get married, and then what will you do?) He would always scream at me: *"Si te veo con un estúpido, lo mato a él primero y después a ti,"* he would say. (If I ever see you with a stupid kid, I will kill him first, and then you.) I am terrified of my dad, but I couldn't stop feeling love for Angel, so I continued my relationship.

After two months, the relationship changed. I was feeling a weird vibe from Angel's close friends. They would laugh like they heard something and wanted to rub it in. I heard rumors and stories from my friends who took classes with him, and why would I doubt their word? I didn't. When I asked him about everything, he was so disappointed with me and told me things that made me feel guilty. I apologized for doubting him.

He was happy for my apology, and the relationship became very nice again. When people saw us, they would shout out, "Cutest couple!" I have to admit I really liked that; anybody would.

One day, after Angel picked me up from class as usual, we were walking when an administrator from the school stopped us. He screamed at me as if I had hit someone. He was spitting in my face every time he screamed, "Give me your ID!" or "What is your name?" I gave him my ID and my name angrily. I walked away very worried and noticed that Angel was worried for me too. He knew that I was going to get in trouble because the administrator wanted to call my house, and he didn't want anything to happen to me. All day I wondered who answered the call. As I was heading home, I got nervous because I didn't know if my father knew or if the message even got to him.

Once I arrived at my house, there were visitors who gave me a look that told me, "Ooh, you are in trouble." At that moment, I knew that my dad knew about the news. A lady in the attendance office had made the phone call, and she had agreed to tell him the things I did in school. I hated her for that. I was lucky that my dad controlled his anger because of the visitors and because I had said, "I shook a guy's hand, and the administrator thought I was holding his hand."

The next day I went to school knowing that it was worth it. I was supposed to see Angel near the P.E. field gate, so when I didn't see him, I wondered why he hadn't come yet. I had something to tell him that I knew would have cheered him up. *Now,* I thought, *I can enjoy the rest of our relationship.* "Oh yay, there he is," I told myself in a soft voice. Out of nowhere, with a serious voice and face, he said the cruelest words, the ones that make your heart beat fast: "I need to talk to you." Then you know something is wrong, and then come the words that end the beating of your heart. "It's over," he said deeply. I had felt it as a dream or a nightmare, but it wasn't, so I cried with so much emotion that nothing would make me stop or feel better.

Relationships are something you can't live with and something you can't live without. You want them and desire them, but you hate them. Girls choose to be with the ones who in the end make them feel bad, and it is their fault. Think before you love. It may be hard, but it is true. Always think before falling for the most beautiful words you can hear. Love is as evil as it is beautiful when it's gone, and that hurts. Once again, ladies, who do we love? The ones who are sweet or the ones who hurt us?

Elba Mendez

YOU CAN DATE HIM, BUT HE'S MINE

Friends are said to come and go, but best friends are forever. I can tell you that for a fact. Best friends are the ones you can turn to without a doubt. A best friend is someone you can hold onto forever—someone you can cry on who will wipe your tears, who will tell you jokes that aren't funny but make you laugh anyway. A best friend is the one who will tell you the truth and bring joy to you anywhere. That person gets the kind of love no one else gets from you. Best friends are just wonderful, and without mine I don't know where I would be.

I have a best friend named Daniel. I've known this guy for three years straight, and those years have been marvelous. He's a very tall, good looking guy…well, for now. His fashion is very nice. His dressy shirts and jeans make him look handsome. I can assure myself that there will always be fun times with him.

We might fight at times, but it's over stupid things. This one time, we didn't talk to each other for about three days straight because I didn't like Ruth, the girl he liked. I didn't approve of her and never would. She broke his heart, I guess, and he was sprung on her. It was just not right. Then one day after school, I was walking by myself, and Daniel was walking behind me with Nicolei. I guess he told her the story of our fight, and she got fed up with it and just screamed, "Geez, Elba, just talk to him already!" We forgave each other, and from that point on, we walked home together.

But most of the time we are always laughing and goofing around. We tend to get in trouble too much, but I guess that's what best friends do. In class we talk and laugh all the time. And no matter how much you try to shut us up, it won't happen. At times people confuse us for a couple, which I think is pretty pathetic. Can't two friends be very close to each other without people thinking they're a couple? I say grow up and live in reality!

Daniel and I have our little adventures outside of school, whether it is walking or just hanging out, like asking for money to go eat together. I love those moments. They're the greatest. I wouldn't trade them for anything in the world. We never have money, so we ask other people who do have money and spend that money wisely. One time we came out of school early and had money and bought a Subway six-inch, two Chiclets, and a can of soda. We sat down, split the sub in half, and shared the soda. We only had about six bucks and were able to buy all those things. They're Kodak moments that I will always remember. I will take them with me to my grave.

We're two for the price of one. We're like salt and pepper, both different but going together. We're inseparable—don't even try. One without the other isn't the same. For example, I went to Mexico for winter break and came back a week after school started, and everyone goes, "Thank God you're back. Daniel hasn't been talking since you've been gone. It's scary." It's just amazing, our friendship. We help each other out in the good and the bad. We embarrass each other, make fun of each other, and love each other. Trust is what counts most, and I know I can trust him for anything.

It's incredible how much I've learned from him. He's the kind of friend you can count on for any occasion. It's funny how I can tell him anything. I guess I see him as a brother. It's just fun being around him, knowing I don't have to worry about any problems or anything like that. Even though he goes to my house and eats my food, I still love him. I'm in a whole different world when I'm with my best friend. Nothing interferes with us. We have ways of being that only we understand. Our jokes and dumb things we do are done for a reason. We get it and think it's funny, even if no one else understands us.

At times he is supportive of my decisions, but most of the time he's not. He doesn't agree with the guys I want to date. He thinks they're not good enough for me, which I guess is a good thing. I guess he's overprotective of me and wants to make sure the guys I date will treat me right. A brother would do the same. He didn't like my piercing, but whether he liked it or not, he got used to it and accepted it. Same as stretching out my earlobe: he didn't like it, but now he is used to it.

Best friends are like family and aren't replaceable. They're one-of-a-kind. And I say if you have a best friend, take care of them and make sure they know how much they mean to you. A best friend will always be there with arms wide open, ready to listen. A best friend is a great gift whom you should really appreciate and love. A best friend will never turn their back on you no matter what. A best friend will stand by you, and I wouldn't trade my friendship with Daniel for anything.

Adriana Escobedo

PANDA BEAR AKA "MY PIOJOSA"

There's a saying from *The Little Rascals* that goes, "You only get one once-in-a-lifetime buddy." You can say just about anything in front of them, and they won't mind listening to you, even if it's boring to them. I have a once-in-a-lifetime buddy, and her name is Pamela. I knew her back in the eighth grade, but we didn't talk much. I had P.E. for fourth period, when Pamela was the teacher's assistant in the girls' locker room. She would always yell at me and rush me to dress up and go to class. I thought she was a mean girl at first until I actually started talking to her in Mr. Payne's algebra class my freshman year of high school. Then we started to get along really well.

Our friendship is unique. It's kind of funny knowing how our friendship grew so fast when we only knew each other for a year and a half. People who just meet us think we hate each other because we love to argue and insult each other most of the time. Actually, we don't really mean what we say. I don't know why, but it's about the only way we show our friendship and love. Our other friends always pick her side when we "argue," but I don't care because I'm only focused on my bestest buddy, Panda Bear. I am amazed how we always argue but never take anything seriously. It may be hard to believe, but we have never gotten mad at each other, not even once. We also love to bug our friend Daniel, even though we get chased around by him (most of the time).

We're both on the soccer team together. She's number 5 and I'm number 22. We always support each other when we're practicing or playing a game against some other high school. There's not a day that goes by without us being seen together. Once, she asked me to come out as a *dama* in her *Quinceañera*, and I felt special because nobody had ever asked me to come out in a *quince* before. The limo may have been too small, and I might have stained my dress with barbecue sauce while Pamela spilled soda all over hers, but everything turned out for the best. We both had lots of fun that day (even though it had some ups and downs), but I believe that brought us closer as friends.

I'd probably be nothing without my Panda Bear. We're always there for each other, like the time she broke up with her ex and I was there to support her. By the time I broke up with that one jerk known as my ex, she was there to help me out and take my mind off him by telling me that I didn't need him. Instead, she told me that I need a big cuddly panda in my life (meaning her, which made me happy).

A best friend is like the sister you could only wish for, somebody who sees you fall to the ground, laughs at you, tries to trip you again, but actually cares for you. Pamela, aka Panda Bear, is one of my best friends, and nobody can ruin our friendship. You can try, but you can't! She's the cookies to my ice cream and the light in my day. We care so much about each other, even though we deny it. I wouldn't trade Pamela for anybody else no matter what. We are P.K., Panda&Kittie, and all you people out there can never come between us.

Aracely Diaz

HAVING A SISTER

I've always wanted a sister. I have my dad, my mom, and my two brothers, but I always felt like there was something missing. There wasn't anyone around to play dolls with me; that's when I realized I was missing a sister. I was always a bit more of a tomboy than a girly-girl because I spent most of my time playing with my brothers. We would spend most of our vacations racing Hot Wheels down ramps we built out of books. I would wrestle with them, but when I wanted to play with my dolls, they weren't interested. My mom would occasionally play with me, but it wasn't the same as another girl. I would always ask my mom for a sister, but the closest thing I ever got to a sister were my friends.

One of my first friends was Thalia. I met her on the very first day of pre-kindergarten. As I walked through what seemed then to be huge crisscrossed gates, I did not want my mom to leave me there. I was afraid because I did not know anyone there, but I was not alone. All of the other kids felt the same way; some of them were even crying and holding onto their moms. As I looked around, I saw many little girls and boys, some with their uniforms on and some without. Most of the girls with uniforms were wearing blue dresses over white collared shirts, white socks, and little black shoes. There was one girl wearing a red Ninja Turtles shirt with sky blue shorts, another wearing a yellow shirt and a blue skirt, and another wearing a green summer dress.

The girl in the green dress stood out to me. I decided to go talk to her because she seemed like the kind of person I would like. I sat next to her in class, and she turned out to be really nice. We became best friends immediately and fortunately had the same teacher in pre-k, kindergarten, and first grade. We would play inside and outside of school; her mom would even invite me to go to the ice-skating rink and the theater with them.

Thalia was a great person; she would always take people to the nurse's office whenever they got hurt on the playground. One day, I was chasing one of my classmates around the rectangular, metal jungle gym when I looked up and was blinded by the sun. That didn't stop me from running and completing my mission. Consequently, I ran into one of the enormous poles and fell to the ground. At that moment I was blind, dizzy, and confused; my head was hurting like never before. But what I remember most about this experience is not the pain but that my best friend Thalia came to me in a heartbeat, showed her concern, and, like always, took me to the nurse. Just as she was starting to feel more like a sister, we got separated. As second grade approached, we had to choose a track; I chose B-track and she chose A-track. I was supposed to go to A-track, but since my brother was in B-track, I was required to go to B-track. I was devastated because I knew that we wouldn't see each other at school anymore, and sooner or later we wouldn't be best friends. The recess schedules for B-track and A-track were different; when I would be on break, she would already have had it. We eventually stopped talking and both made new best friends.

From second grade through fifth grade, my best friend was Kimberly. She was a Filipina with dark skin, straight black hair, and dark brown eyes. We would go to each other's houses often since we lived a block and a half away from each other. Since we had known each other for four years already and we both only had brothers, we were like sisters. What I remember most about my friendship with Kimberly is that we would always play handball, whether it be at school, my house, or her house. We would stay after school; I would bring the red rubber ball, and we would play on the yellow wall with the painted blue eagle mascot. There were two benches on the side of the court, and people would come up to challenge us. We were the champions of handball in our class because we played so much.

However, I also stopped being friends with Kimberly. This time it was not because it was nearly impossible to see each other but because she changed a lot during middle school, and in the end we just drifted apart. I really tried to maintain a friendship with her, but she wanted to hang out with other people. Most of the time I was the one who would call and try to keep in touch, but she didn't put much effort into it. I got tired of being the only one trying so I just stopped.

As the years passed, I was no longer interested in having a sister. As I grew up, my interests in playing with dolls faded. I always wondered what it would have been like to have a sister in my home life, though, and now I have an idea of how it feels. My brother's girlfriend of five years, Aillyn, and I have become so close I feel as if she were my real older sister. She is always there if I need her, she invites me to many places and buys me things, and she really cares about me. I feel and do the same for her. One of the main reasons we are so close is that she practically saw me grow up because she met me when I was in fifth grade. I can still remember when we met; I was a bit shorter than her, but as the years passed I became taller.

As the years have gone by and my desire for a sister has slowly diminished, I now have a friend whom I consider a sister. I have grown attached to Aillyn and will always think of her as a sister. I feel like I can always count on her. Even if my brother and Aillyn break up, there is not a chance that I will stop talking to her. I know that she would continue seeing me as her little sister, and for that I will always look at her as my big sister.

Mariana Kouloumian

WHO TO TRUST

When I was in middle school, a very close friend of mine decided to suddenly put an end to our friendship. Ending a long friendship isn't easy, at least for me. I still remember the weather, the clothing I was wearing, and everything that was going on. It was a sunny day at school, and as usual, kids were running around. I was sitting on a bench and waiting for my friend.

The day before, another girl called me and said, "She doesn't want to be your friend anymore and she's never liked you and you don't mean anything to her." I really didn't pay attention to it because I figured it was just a joke they were playing on me, but I still wanted to make sure. As she approached me, I looked up at her and said with a low voice, "Why? Why are you doing this?"

She responded, "I never liked you. I don't want to like you, and I want to end this friendship." I was shocked. I couldn't believe it. Here was a girl I was always there for whenever she needed someone to talk to and when she felt alone in the world—like no one listened to her. I was by her side, but I guess she forgot that and put an end to our friendship. I just walked away and that was that.

Throughout that time, all I could think was, *What now? If this happened, then is friendship real?* My parents were the only people whom I could go to. They understood how I felt and the things I was going through. It's amazing how you think your friend is always going to be there and always understand you, when in the end, your mom is your best friend.

I told my mom what I was going through, and she told me, "It's OK; if she let someone like you slip from her hands, then she isn't worth you being there for her." My parents told me that life is filled with many obstacles and happy memories. The choices you make become the future you choose. My parents always believed in me and showed me right from wrong. Without them and their lectures and words of encouragement, I would probably end up alone. I strongly believe parents mend their children and push them to be their best. The older you become, the wiser you get and the more you know. A ten-year-old's brain is very different than an eighteen-year-old's brain.

As I look at the past, there are many things I would've done differently if I had gone to my family instead of my friends for advice. Having a parent in your life gives you a sense of security, knowing someone will always love you no matter what.

As a fifteen-year-old girl, I can't say I've gone through many things in my life—because I haven't yet. I don't know how it feels to be alone and have no one by my side, and I thank God every day for giving me an amazing family that lets me correct my mistakes and stands behind me all the way. My parents have always taught me to be strong, to let no one get to me, and to always think two steps ahead before making a decision. An intelligent man once told me that if your parents aren't making you mad at least four times a week, then they're not doing their job. I believe that and think it's parents' jobs to be on your case and ask questions.

I think parents are there to help you grow and mend your life, and they do have power over you. My parents are the reason why I wake up every morning and come to school. They're the reason I make the right choices and have big goals and dreams. Being a teenager in this generation is very hard; you go through so many things that you can't handle, and it's hard when there is no one there to point you in the right direction. Life is what you make out of it. It's the memories you make and the happiness you form. You need a mom's love and a dad's encouragement. No one can tell you how to live your life, but you need to have a smart head on your shoulders so you won't go heading down the wrong road. I'm thankful for having parents who care and always give me the advice I need to get through my troubles. My family has helped me overcome every problem or obstacle I have faced, and I'm glad for that.

My parents always expect the best of me, and I can never handle the disappointed look on their faces when I do something wrong, or be OK with upsetting them. Many teenagers these days don't appreciate what they have or realize how thankful they should be for having a family. Some kids long for the warmth of having a family and want a chance to be loved, while others take advantage of their loved ones and treat them like they're nothing. Family matters a lot to me; I guess I'm one of those people who needs that feeling of warmth and to be surrounded by people who love me. My family has made a huge impact on my life.

If I didn't have amazing parents, I wouldn't be the person I am today. There have been many times in my life when I needed advice or someone to talk to, and no one was around. I felt embarrassed to go to my parents and talk to them, but I realized that the smartest advice I can get is from them. Many people have told me to never ask for advice from people my own age. I agree. People my age tend to give me the advice I want to hear, not the advice that's going to help me out. Asking people many years older than you is better because they have gone through more than you.

In the end, I rely on my family because they've always been there for me and always will be. As for my old friend, I actually forgave her, and now we are friends again. She apologized and had no idea why she had done that. My parents have taught me to love my enemies more and forgive their mistakes to help make them better people. I forgave her, but now I know whom to trust and what to do or not to do.

Aram Gambourian

THE ENCOUNTER ON A SATURDAY MORNING

The day was a beautiful Saturday morning when the birds were chirping, the squirrels were playing, and the sun was shining. As I stumbled from my room to the living room, a stream of sunlight momentarily blinded me, and I bumped my foot on the coffee table. I quickly recovered and lay down on the couch. A couple of minutes passed before my sister joined me in the living room to watch TV.

Right then I started to hear voices coming from outside, and I thought it was the neighborhood kids playing, so I ignored it. My sister, always the curious one in the family, looked outside through the window. She quickly shouted at me, telling me to come see what was going on outside. My mom was chasing a middle-aged white lady in my front yard down the stairs, through the gate, and onto the street.

I raced to my room, where I frantically changed my clothes, but I couldn't find my shoes. My room was a mess—I had clothes piled up so high I thought I was on Mt. Ararat. I found my shoes under my bed. I quickly put them on and rushed to the front door. Just when I was about to open the door, I saw my mother, who looked really infuriated—the vein in her neck was popping out, her hair (usually straight) seemed wavy, and her short stature seemed intimidating. She came in, sat down on the couch, and told us what happened.

"I was watering the plants on the side of the house with your brother," she explained. "I came around the corner and I saw a dark figure behind the lemon tree. I gave the hose to your brother and went to investigate what that mysterious figure was. When I walked around the tulips to the lemon tree, I saw a white lady ripping and plucking off petals from the rosebushes. I asked her who the hell she was and told her to leave. She turned around and gave me the finger. I asked her

16

again who the hell she was and what the hell she was doing. She turned around and gave me the finger again. I just snapped and warned her that I was going to call the police. She then looked at the front door to my house, and I thought that you guys might be in danger."

My mom told us that the woman was of average build and had a wrinkled face, long dirty blonde hair, eyes like an owl's, and one big mole on her face just like a witch. A real witch—right out of a horror story.

Our family owns a four-unit complex in Hollywood. Mary, one of our tenants, came out because she saw what was happening from her apartment on the second floor. Mary came outside to back up my mom and warned the intruder that they were going to call the police.

The white lady turned around and said, "This building is now mine and I can do whatever I want. I inherited this building from my grandmother when she died a week ago. You better leave now before I make you."

My mother had enough and brought out the big guns. She furiously walked up to the balcony and grabbed the golf club. As she walked clown the stairs, the lady stared at her. My mother thought she might have gotten drunk at Jumbo's Clown Room, the gentlemen's club next to us, but she didn't care what the reason was. My mother walked up to her, golf club in hand, raised like a bat ready to swing. When the lady saw my mother, she started walking backwards down the stairs, through the gate, and out to the street very slowly, while still cursing at Mary and my mother. My mother got close enough and swung at her. She missed intentionally to scare her away, not to hurt her. The lady turned around and ran down the sidewalk with my mother chasing her out to the middle of the street. Afterward, my mother walked up to the balcony, put the golf club away, and came into the house. Mary went home, still thinking about what happened.

We never saw the white lady again. Later that night, my grandma, my family, and Mary's family met in the back balcony to drink coffee. We retold the story and laughed.

This made me think that mothers react intuitively without thinking when their children are in danger. My mother told me, "I am your mother, protector, and friend." I realized that my mother is willing to do anything for us, her children, to be safe, and she will do anything to save her flowers.

Maura

ZERO TO HERO

As little girls we all grow up idolizing our dads. We say to our friends, "My dad's the best. He knows every thing there is to know." But with some girls that isn't the case. Living in Los Angeles with both of my parents, I thought I had a wonderful life. As I grew older, though, I started to feel this awful hate for my father. It all started somewhere around the age of six. I know, what a young age, right? There was a reason for what was starting to come over me: my dad started drinking when I was five. At first it was normal. He would have a drink or two, and then he would fall asleep. It never got out of hand until my younger brother Edin was born. Then my dad would come home drunk every day and would make a mess in our house. At first I thought he probably had more than two drinks that night, and it would be a one-time thing, but that wasn't the case. He kept coming home drunk and was getting out of hand.

One night he started fighting with my mom for no reason and yelled at me to take my little brother out of the room. I have to admit that I was really scared of my dad that night. I've never seen my dad react so violently towards anyone, and that one night he wasn't just violent toward my mom, but he was violent toward me. Even though it wasn't physical, that night marked my life. Things got worse and worse after that. Not only was he reckless but he stopped coming home at night and wouldn't come back until the next day. His drinking got to a point that my mom decided to move us out of the house. The first time we moved out, we went to live with my Aunt Concha.

It felt like all of the mishaps in my life were because of my dad. After only one month my parents got back together, and we moved back into the house. Things were fine for a few weeks until one day the nightmare came back. At first I didn't expect him to get so out of hand, but he did and that was the final straw for my mom and me. That night things got so out of hand that for the first time ever I saw my dad physically attack my mom. It was the worst thing I've ever witnessed in my entire life. Just hearing my mom scream for help and not being able to do anything to help her made me feel so useless. I felt that their fight was my fault, and that I was the one to blame for everything. I can't explain the feeling of watching someone attack my mom; it's the worst feeling in the world. Apparently that was the last straw for my mom, and we moved out again. This time we moved in with my Aunt Marisa. My dad kept trying to win my mom back, but it didn't work. The times I saw my dad, I would feel so much hate for him that it got to a point that I was scared to give him a hug or even to talk to him. I think that in a way I was traumatized by what I saw as a young girl. Watching my dad beat my mom isn't an easy thing to forget.

Thankfully, my dad decided to seek help for his drinking problem. The last time I ever saw my dad drink alcohol was about eleven years ago, and the last time I saw him lay his hand on my mom was about eleven years ago, too. For a person to get rid of a drinking problem is very difficult, and for them to actually admit they have one says a lot about their personality. That's the reason why I now look at my dad as a different man from who he was when I was five or six years old. At the age of sixteen I realized that people make mistakes; that's what makes them human. Admitting the mistake and trying to fix it is what makes them admirable people. When I was six I saw my dad as the most despicable person on the earth; now that I'm sixteen, he's one of my idols.

Leslie Cerda-Lopez

LESSONS LEARNED

Ever since I was a small child, my mom did all the chores around the house. She always went to the market without help from anyone and had food ready for us when my sister and I would arrive home from school, or when my dad would get home from a long day at work as a waiter. My mom was capable of doing all of this and working by herself, too. She would work for a little while in the morning, then come home. My mom would buy my eleven-year-old sister and me anything we wanted, even though it wasn't necessary. But all of this changed unexpectedly.

On May 5, 2006, my mother had an accident. She was hiking in the mountains with my dad, and on their way back down she slipped. My dad had to carry her all the way down the mountain because she was in so much pain. We discovered she had fractured two bones in her left leg.

Ever since that day, everything in my home was different than how it had been before. Obviously, my mom couldn't do much because of her leg. Now, it was my turn to be mom. Every day, I would wake up at 5:30 a.m. to get ready and make breakfast for everyone in my family: my dad, my mom, and my sister.

I would come home from school and cook for my family, who would complain about my food.

"It doesn't taste good."

"It's not cooked well enough."

"You left it on the stove too long."

"There's not enough salt."

"There's too much salt."

It was a headache!

20

One time, I cooked *carne asada*, a dish my mother made a lot. It is cooked on the stove over a medium flame. First, a tomato is cut into small pieces and put in the pot. While it cooks a little, the onions are added, and finally the meat. When I finished, I thought I did a great job. I was surprised!

But when I cut into the meat, it was still red.

I thought, "OK, maybe this is the only problem; I should have just cooked it a little more, but it's OK."

So, I took a bite. It tasted horrible! I realized how bad a cook I actually was. It tasted nothing like meat. It was so embarrassing. But how was I magically supposed to know how to cook if my mom never taught me how?

I also had to clean the house, including the bathroom, which I thought was gross because it meant cleaning the toilet as well. If I didn't do my chores right, my dad would get mad. I guess it was because we were so used to seeing my mom do everything perfectly. I had never done any of these things before, so I was stressed out. To make things worse, my mom lost her job and I no longer got whatever I wanted. My dad would only buy me stuff I really needed and not stuff that I just wanted.

There was screaming, slamming doors, and arguing in my house practically all the time. I regret not ever actually helping my mom with the chores: cleaning the bathroom, washing dishes, doing laundry, going to the market, cooking meals, and making beds. When my mom was recovering, I had to learn how to do all these things. I realized how difficult her life was. She has to do whatever she can to be a great mom. And she is.

I learned a lot from that experience. I think if kids are in a situation like I was, where their mom does everything for them, they should help and appreciate their mom. Everything may look easy, but once you're the one doing it you realize it's not. I also learned that I shouldn't be so greedy and only ask my parents to buy me stuff I really need.

Now, I do chores in my house without a problem and enjoy doing them, too. My dad gives me a little extra money for being a great example to my little sister. My cooking has gotten better now—the meat I make actually tastes like meat!

Kevin Guevara

BECOMING A BETTER PERSON

When I was seven, my grandfather and I used to have conversations about how I could become a better person. We sat under a tree on a wooden bench and talked until sunset about me and about his life in El Salvador. I remember him every time I see the picture of him before I step out of the house.

My grandfather was a wise old man who had lived it all. He was a well-respected man, and everyone loved him. He used to be involved in military hardware supplies for our country. In El Salvador there was a lot of poverty, and my grandfather used to help people by supplying them with food, money, clothes, and diapers.

In times of war, people didn't have money or food for themselves or their children. During El Salvador's civil war, milk was very expensive, and only wealthy people could afford it. My grandfather distributed milk to the villages so people who didn't even have a loaf of bread to eat would have food to give their children.

His favorite quote was "God gives to the giver and takes from the taker." This quote makes me think hard and review its meaning. To me, it means that if you are a giving person, people will give you something in return. As an example, if a person gave a hundred dollars to a person in need, then a hundred dollars would come back to them; but if a person takes a hundred dollars from another, then that person would have a hundred dollars taken away from them.

The quote also makes me feel things more deeply. I feel for others who are in need, and because of their needs I give them what I can. If anytime, anywhere I see a homeless person, I look around to see who would help except for me. There isn't anybody. I take it upon myself to help and give them what they need. If it is a cold day, I buy hot drinks to make them warm. If it is a hot day, I buy them water to quench their thirst.

People are surprised by my kindness; it isn't hard to care for someone besides yourself. Be kind and generous without the thought of receiving something in return. We should help our community so we can live in a good society and make the earth a better place. I think that when your eye catches someone who is going through a rough time, you should help them so that we can all become better people.

Becky De Leon

POLLUTION ON MOTHER EARTH

After the school bell rings, I see bottles, cans, chip bags, and chewing gum on the floor around campus. This makes me feel as if society has become very dirty. There have been a few times I have stepped or sat on some repugnant substance that lay on the floor. When I ask people, "Why don't you pick up your trash?" they respond, "Because the janitor can pick it up." People don't realize that if a piece of trash is picked up by the wind it will affect our world in drastic ways.

It seems to me that just about everywhere our environment is getting polluted. People don't realize this is destroying our world and leading to disasters. This means our loved ones from around the globe are also doomed. This makes me scared, too, because in Guatemala I have family, including a brother whom I love very much, and I wouldn't know what to do if anything were to happen to them. I am hoping to visit them, but with our world polluted, one day we might not be able to easily go to another country because there could be some devastating changes. Whatever it may be, I don't think it would be a favorable change.

In biology class, I learned there are many types of pollution, including air, ocean, and land pollution. It is devastating that there is not a spot on Earth that isn't polluted. Factories are one of the main sources of pollution in both the air and the ocean. This and many other things are threatening existence on Mother Earth.

Ever since I learned what pollution has caused the planet, I have changed my behavior. I throw my trash where it belongs, in the trash can. I also recycle bottles and cans, and remind people to pick up after themselves. I believe it is wrong to not throw trash where it belongs. Manners are something you learn as a little kid, and picking up after yourself is one of them.

I also learned to be considerate of others' feelings and personal space. There are other living organisms that we affect when our pollution causes disturbances in their ecosystems. Many people don't believe this will really affect their lifetimes, but if we disturb the habitats of other organisms it will bounce back to us in a dramatic way.

Larry Dubois

It was two weeks after my sixteenth birthday, or two weeks before; I'm not sure. I took my first breath of the air that filled the dimly lit liquor store on the day I will always remember. It was a day when the sun cast a tinge of haziness—a golden-yellow beam through the window—in the direction of the only thing that was on my mind at the time: the shamrock-green bottle of Perrier sparkling water in the cooler. After catching a glimpse of the bottle, I turned to my long-time friend (I'll call him Rick) and asked him how much he liked sparkling water. (At this point, however, my mind was already fixed on buying it.) He confided in me that if we were to buy it, his dollar would be well spent. So we went ahead and picked out two lemon-flavored fizzy waters, both a liter in size. We promptly paid and left the premises.

Our destination? School. You see, the year up to this point was a painful blessing that nagged on. It was as though I had given up all I had ever been taught, living lost in a sea of hopeless individuals for whom there was no recovery. Like many of my peers, I was locked in a trap that appeared inescapable. I had grown tired after I figured it had gone on for long enough. Something in my mind told me to hoist myself back onto my feet and stand tall.

I devised a plan on the spot with the approval of Rick: we would exit the institution that caused this deep pain. Not that it was the school's fault, but before school, all was well. Quiet. Tranquil. Our lives were balanced.

My mom brought a tradition to our family, one of a couple we practiced on New Year's Eve. "Write the bad parts about the year on one side of the paper, Larry," she would say. "Then, on the other, write the change you want to come."

I wrote mine out, along with my mom and dad, but we didn't reveal them to each other, like a wish before extinguishing a set of birthday candles. We threw them into the fire and watched them burn.

Now, my plan was devised, and I had already let Rick in on my idea. He agreed. My body grew tense as I turned to Rick and asked him if he was ready. "You bet," he replied. We both squeezed the necks of the bottles and threw them as hard as we could into our "beloved" institution. Mine landed first and made the most incredible POP! I had ever imagined. It was as if the bottle contained too much energy to just crash and break. It exploded. It let go. Just like I had let go. It was one of the most beautiful moments in my young life. There I was, tall, replenished and in the middle of the biggest grin. Boy, was I grateful. I pulled in a deep breath of air and we both took off running running running running like there was no tomorrow, but soon all we could do was walk in silence, amazed by the graciousness that had just revealed itself to our lost souls. We embraced it. We both still carry this day with us.

No one may ever understand, and that's OK. The point wasn't to make others understand how a bad judgment changed our lives. It's alright. I was on the edge of the boat, soaking up the world, and it was great. Now I'm back. Good old me, you know. So take the chance and burn the paper, throw the bottle; it doesn't matter. Just don't give up hope, because you're going to figure it out when the fire burns out and the janitor finishes picking up the last bits of glass.

Jose Batres

ON THE WAY HOME FOR THE WEEKEND

I stare intently at the time. My eyes can't leave my watch. It is Friday, sixth period, with three more minutes until the bell rings and I can go home. It was a fun day at school today, but I want my weekend to start already. I feel good about the weekend. The bell rings, and I feel a weight lift off my shoulders. My heart skips a beat and my head actually feels lighter. I walk out of my classroom into a hallway filled with hundreds of students, laughing, screaming, jumping, and talking with so much joy. As I walk out of the building, I see more students. Students wait for the bus, wait for their parents, and make phone calls. They are loud, but they are happier to be outside than inside. Security guards and administrators look for any after-school trouble. I feel protected.

Finally, my older cousin picks up my brother, my cousin, and me. I look outside the car window and see the sky. It's blue with white clouds. As we get closer to my home, the clouds become different shapes and look like they are moving with the car. When we are on different streets and get different views, I can see the Hollywood sign and the observatory in the mountains. I know I'm getting closer to my house.

I see more students walking home with their friends. They are laughing, fooling around with each other. Some of these students look tired because of the long walk home. Some students are sitting, waiting on bus stop benches. Some listen to music; others read books so they don't get bored. As I get closer and closer to my home, the streets change. There are more apartment buildings than houses where I live. I finally see my building.

I stand still for a moment and listen. Around me I can hear the birds chirping, the dogs growling, and the cars speeding away. I smell the polluted air from all the cars. Yuck! I want to smell fresh air for once. I wonder if pollution is ever going to stop, but we need cars for transportation and factories to make things.

Outside my building different kinds of cars are parked on the streets: Hondas, Acuras, and Mustangs. Some look fancy and some look old. Also, I see a handful of students arriving at their homes around where I live. They look tired. They are sweating, like they just want something to drink. I am so lucky to get a ride from school to my house because it is a pretty long walk.

Finally, I go inside my building. Wow—it doesn't look that old from the outside, but when I climb the red stairs it starts to look really old. The carpet is brown with marks on it. My building has five floors and covers two streets. My uncle and his wife live there, too, as do my immediate family and my cousin, the one who picks me up from school. My neighbors are all cool, except for one couple that lives on our floor. They always say we make too much noise.

I walk down the hallways, climb the stairs, and knock on my front door. My mom opens. I scream out, "Home, home, home!" At last, I can use my computer to chat with my friends, play games, and just have fun. I can even call my friends to see if they want to go somewhere to hang out, and not even think about or mention school. Or I can just watch TV. Total relaxation and comfort. Who wouldn't pay at least $25 for this precious moment?

On the trip home, I notice what my city, Los Angeles, looks like, how my community is, and how many things we have to do for fun. I also get to see some of the bad things we have like pollution. One day I am going to tell my cousin not to pick me up so I can see things I can't see from a car.

Stephanie Fuentes

WHAT A FRIDAY!

I was in class bored and tired; I kept looking at the clock and counting down the seconds until we got out of school. Five, four, three, two, ding went the bell at exactly 3:13 p.m.

"Finally it's Friday!" I yelled. I couldn't wait to get out of school. I was eager to get home and sleep or do anything other than learn, but I knew that was going to be impossible. That whole week I had been making plans to lie on the sofa and stuff my face with popcorn, candy, and all the other types of junk food I'd discovered in the past fifteen years of my life. I was so excited! I told my best friend that I was going to be lazy the whole weekend. My friend told me we had homework. At that moment, I felt like a car that had just been stopped by a never-ending red light. I was furious! One minute you might be living your dream, but when that minute passes you might lose everything.

I started walking to my grandma's car and thinking about my homework. I don't know why, but I was distracted by all the questions in my head when out of nowhere BAM! I crashed into a big telephone pole! Across the street, an older woman was laughing at me and telling me my face was red. I ran to my grandma's car and looked in the mirror, and there they were, two splinters that looked like zits on my forehead. I didn't know what to do. I was thinking about the dumbest things: Was I going to survive? What if the splinter went into my brain? I finally got home alive, but my grandma was still laughing at me.

As I was walking towards my apartment, I saw an ugly repainted door that was a weird blue. "Oh my God," I yelled as I got closer and saw that it was my apartment door. The others around it were the same. I saw the manager, and he was singing "Wouldn't It Be Nice" by the Beach Boys. As I walked by him he was giving himself compliments on how great the doors looked, and for some reason he was hiding his head in a bandanna.

He was using phrases such as "groovy" and "right on" and saying how he wanted to "roll with the homies." At that moment I knew something wasn't right so I went back to say hi. He got up from where he was sitting, took off his bandanna, and said, "*Hola* Yennifer, I mean Estephanie. How are you?" When his bandanna came off I couldn't help but laugh at the new hairpiece that he was wearing. I know I should have just replied and said hi back but it just was so funny. His hairpiece looked like someone ran over a poor squirrel and then sold it to him. It was awful; it actually had a tail that was two different colors. But it went great with what he was wearing: a bright sky-blue tank top with bright red short shorts and long knee-high socks that had two red and green stripes at the top.

I thought he was in a mid-life crisis. I ran into my house to call my mom, but I couldn't get hold of her; she was either busy or in a meeting. When I went outside again I saw him with his wife, who looked very nice. I would say she looked professional. She began yelling at him in Spanish but then said "Francisco, I understand your favorite color is blue, but can you please paint the doors their original color?" After that she mumbled curse words in Spanish. I was in shock. Here was the man who was always walking and talking tough, threatening people and telling them that they better pay their rent on time, and he was acting like a dead-scared Mexican Chihuahua. "Wow. What a man," I said to myself as I giggled all the way back to my house. After all that commotion that Friday, I couldn't wait for Saturday. When the day came, though, it was pretty boring. While talking on the phone with my best friend, Maura, I told her what happened, and she laughed. I told her that Friday taught me a few lessons: never think when you're walking, try to avoid large telephone poles, and if you ever see the manager of your apartment wearing something repulsive, talk to him and his wife—it'll make a whole lot of funny drama.

Rebecca Bowden

MY SECOND HOME

Almost every week I have the privilege of witnessing my beautiful, gleaming downtown Los Angeles transition into a flat, yellow, barren landscape. This transition takes place over a dreadful ninety-minute car ride that eventually ends in a town called Lancaster.

Lancaster is a place that prides itself on its color-coordinated strip malls, identical stucco houses, and almost non-existent population; a white-trash oasis where people are allowed the glamour of saying they live in Los Angeles while enjoying the comforts of an all-white community. Its inhabitants are allowed an escape from the world, where they can spend their days buying "Support Our Troops" bumper stickers and debating last night's PTA meeting. People venture outside of Lancaster only to visit the beach or, occasionally, the Grand Canyon, and people venture into Lancaster only when they have no choice or are as deranged as my family.

My grandmother (or "Nana," as I was trained to call her) lives in a large, one-story house across from a vast field of yellowing, thorny weeds. The outside of the house has the potential to be what some people would call "nice" if it weren't for the grease-stained driveway or the presence of countless pieces of old scrap wood and furniture in the front yard. The house's exterior gives anyone who walks by a clear picture of its insides and the people who live there.

The interior of the house includes off-white textured walls complete with fading crayon marks and a stained magenta carpet covered with broken bits of toys and dog hair. Most of these walls are covered by shelves supporting dolls, quilts, and dozens of antique clocks that provide the house with a loud, constant ticking sound (which stands as a constant reminder of the valuable time being spent there).

In the middle of the living room are two green, pillowless couches (the pillows always manage to end up on the floor) that are divided by an ornate, 80s glass coffee table that supports as many dirty dishes as possible without collapsing. Besides these three items, almost every other piece of furniture (or object) in the house has a price tag, ready for my grandmother to sell and ship to another suburban mom in a different part of the country.

My grandmother's appearance can easily be compared to that of an ogre. She is a large (but not fat) woman of forty-eight whose wardrobe is never complete without some type of bell-sleeved, dainty floral top with bright white Skechers. Her graying brown hair is always pinned back with two bobby pins, giving her the look of an over-aged junior high student. Because of her size, she has the habit of waddling wherever she goes.

My grandmother refers to herself as an "antique merchant." Most of her sales take place on eBay, where what she auctions off is not determined by whether it belongs to her, but by whether it can fit in a cardboard shipping box. Most of her sales consist of items she buys at garage sales, or presents, already given to one of her children the previous Christmas or birthday, and now taken back. Her "selling off the house" (as my grandfather calls it) is probably due to her rigorous thriftiness. Once, when I was about nine, we were birthday shopping for a friend when I asked her for a Barbie furniture set I had seen on the shelf. I quickly realized I was wrong for doing so when my grandmother, in a hurried and almost hysterical tone, erupted into an explanation of her entire current financial status and why she couldn't buy me the toy. After listening to a ten-minute lecture on my grandparents' fiscal history I finally interrupted and told her, "You could have just said no."

To this day I am reluctant to bring up anything that might ignite one of my grandmother's melodramatic, self-pitying speeches. However, she thrives on martyrdom and will use any opportunity to highlight the horrible acts of hatred her children have committed against her. Just a few months ago she discovered her tape dispenser was missing. Before attempting to find it, my grandmother began a theatrical scene where she cried out in rage that her kids had stolen said tape dispenser in an attempt to keep her from her eBay work. No one understood the connection between tape and eBay, nor did they care. Her relentless paranoia and theories of sabotage did not end there. According to my grandmother, one of my aunts had taught the dog to poop in the house just so she would step in it, and the other had thrown trash under the bed for my grandmother to clean in order to "punish" her for not liking the dog. Overall, when adding up my "Nana's" positive attributes, I am not surprised by her choice of a mate.

From the time I was born, my grandmother insisted that I call my step-grandfather "Papa"—a name that now disturbs me considering my mother and several people outside of our family refer to him as "The Seventies Movie Star." Many have theorized that what gives him this sleazy, eccentric appearance are his chiseled nose and distinct, thick black mustache that reaches to the tip of his lip. What disturbs me most about this reference is that my grandfather is aware of it and seems to be flattered that someone has made the comparison. After being reminded of his eccentric appearance, he always proceeds to tell whoever is listening that he was used several times as a police decoy for catching similar-looking seedy criminals.

Because of my lack of knowledge of seventies films, I always thought he looked like the stereotypical cop—which he is. He carries all the qualities of the despised police officer: racist, conservative, and obsessive. My grandfather is so obsessed with his job, in fact, that he's on the lookout for crime even when he's off duty. One day while he was taking me and my aunts (who are both in elementary school—a result of our family tradition of teen pregnancy) for an after-school snack at the local Arco, he witnessed a group of boys running across the street without using the crosswalk, some of whom happened to be classmates of mine. He began to yell at them for committing such a heinous crime. His scolding persisted for more than five of the most mortifying minutes of my life. But I had to forgive him; he was protecting the law-abiding citizens of Lancaster from those evil jaywalkers. "Papa" invests a lot in Lancaster; he loves it there. He vigorously helps the community, participating in elementary school politics, helping out backstage at dance recitals, and, most importantly, acting as President of the Antelope Valley Children's Choir. For the past ten years he has been organizing the choir with thirty fat, middle-aged mothers wearing tie-dye T-shirts or Winnie the Pooh overall dresses. His passion for extracurricular activities amazes me.

The products of this amazing couple are two Lancasterians, born and bred. The older, Samantha, is eleven—an age where Lancaster's narrow-minded and conservative influence is irreversible and embedded into every thought produced under her thin, blonde hair. For Emily, who is seven years old, there is still hope, although opportunities to save her are few. Both already show symptoms of what could very well lead them to a long life of tract homes, mini vans, and capri pants. For now, they continue their suburban cultural development while sitting on the couch at all hours of the day with a Game Boy glued to one hand and a bag of chips in the other. Both are unresponsive as "Nana" shouts curses and threats begging them to do the most minor of chores. I leave these scenes of insanity knowing comfort will slowly return to me as I transition back home into Los Angeles. Once I am given this temporary relief from the Lancastriac chaos, I merely spend it anticipating my next car ride to the flat yellowness that never seems to leave my mind completely.

Marlon Huiza

MY EXPERIENCES IN INDEPENDENCE

It was five thirty in the morning when my mom and I arrived in Kansas City, Missouri. Little did I know I was going to have the worst three-and-a-half years of my life in the little town we were moving to: Independence. It was a beautiful place with grass, lots of trees, and not much traffic. The air was clean, rich and thick to breathe, and the girls in Independence were hotter than the girls I had known back in Los Angeles. It seemed like a great, peaceful place to live—but I did not know the history behind that little town in Missouri.

After I had settled in and started fifth grade, eight months flew by in the blink of an eye. Three weeks into sixth grade, I met a very cool, funny, and bright kid named Dante Jones. He had this ability to know when someone was down and bring him back up again by saying or doing something funny. I got to meet his family—Danna, Frank, and Danisha—the day of the parent conference in October, and his mom invited me to go to his house one day after school. After that, I would go to his house about once a week to hang out with his Labrador retriever Polo and play basketball and PlayStation 2. Dante and I became really close, almost like brothers, despite the fact that we weren't the same race.

The day before Thanksgiving, I received a phone call from Dante asking me if I wanted to go to his grandma's house with three other friends. When we got there, Teron, T.J., Monte, and I got the opportunity to listen to Dante's grandma's stories about living in the darkest days of prejudice and racism. She explained what it was like to live in fear of people who would kill any black person they saw walking at night, and told us about how hard it was to raise fifteen kids while making about two dollars a day selling fruit on the streets. After hearing her stories, a huge chill

35

ran down my spine as I imagined living in that period of time, trying to survive the harsh and cruel punishments being inflicted upon me and the blacks. Hearing her stories made me feel like crying, and when I looked around, I saw Teron, T.J., Monte, and Dante in tears, all of us feeling bad about how some people's behaviors could frighten other people for good.

Though we did not experience the life of Dante's grandma, Dante and I had our own experiences with racism. Once I stepped into seventh grade, the white skater friends I had hung out with before turned very racist against me, Dante, and other black and Mexican kids. The trouble really started when a lot of Mexican kids moved to Independence. I started to hang out with some of them who were not the kind of people you would want to mess with. They were pretty funny, but when it came down to business, they put on a serious look that made you not even try to stare at them.

Fights happened a lot in seventh grade, with the blacks and Mexicans on one side and the racist whites on the other. Day after day, week after week, month after month, someone would get jumped and beat up badly. Soon there were a lot of racist white kids—enough to beat up everyone on campus—and I was one terrified kid, because I was scared that I might get jumped. The blacks, Mexicans, and the white skaters who were not racist had our backs, but we couldn't count on them to be wherever we were.

There were a few lucky ones who did not get jumped, but Dante and I got beat up a couple of times. Dante would come home acting weird and scared, and his mom could tell that something was wrong. But my mom never noticed because I would cover up my swollen and busted-up face when I came home. Seventh grade was a total nightmare for me. It was a long, dark year.

The tension between the whites and the blacks and Mexicans cooled down a little when I started the eighth grade because some of the kids involved asked themselves what the point in this was. However, some kids did not change. The Mexicans that I knew went back to LA to do their own thing, and the blacks got bigger, buffer, and tougher. I had a friend named Aaron Rimsen who was the baddest kid I knew because he knew how to fight. He could take out four people simultaneously, or so I'd heard.

There wasn't as much racist fighting as before, but some still happened: throughout eighth grade, I was only jumped twice. I was brave enough to fight back but couldn't protect myself because I was small and weak. However, one of my skater friends, Stephen Gunderson, told me it didn't matter how hard you hit, it was how hard you could take it and still get back on your feet. That gave me the strength and courage to walk into school. Every day as I walked into that building I had the courage to take as many punches as I could. Beat up or not, I would keep going to class and trying to do my work, so I was not brought down.

When eighth grade was over, a lot of the kids changed and started enjoying life rather than being angry all the time. My mom and I moved back to Los Angeles where I have found my real family—the friends I grew up with before I moved. LA is my home because there are many different kinds of people living here: Asians, blacks, Hispanics, whites, Armenians, Hindus, and many more. By talking to people with different cultural backgrounds than me, I can learn something about them—stuff I wouldn't learn by living somewhere with only one or two different kinds of people. Los Angeles is my real home, where I don't have to deal with racism.

Aurea Paraiso

OUT OF PLACE

There are times in your life when you face dramatic changes. For me, it's moving. I was born in the US but raised in the Philippines while my mother, father, and big sister were in America. My parents had to work every day so they didn't have time to take care of us. My aunts and uncles raised my sister, brother, and me in a small house made of wood that could have been shattered by a hurricane. Living with them was rough. They treated us like slaves. We did everything we were asked to do because we had no choice. We were scared, and we would try to avoid getting hit, but we would still get beaten. That was life.

When I grew older I had more responsibilities, but I was still only eight. I was confused and afraid about what was going on in my life. I started to feel out of place. One day my uncle and aunt brought me to the Philippine Embassy in Manila. They took pictures of me and took my fingerprints. I had never done that before. I realized that I was going somewhere, somewhere far without my brother and sister, but after we went back to our village I forgot all about it.

A few months later my aunt told me my passport was completed and that my Tita Ellen was going to pick me up. I was going to America. I was shocked. I didn't want to leave my brother and sister. I couldn't possibly go without them! Before I left, my brother said, "*Ate Janne, puwede ba akong sumama sayo?*" ("Big sister Janne, can I go with you?") My brother wanted to go inside my bag, which made me feel sadder. Saying good-bye was the hardest part.

After a long flight, we finally arrived at the airport in Los Angeles. The weather in the Philippines was always hot, but here it was cold. I felt lonely and afraid. I saw my mother, father, and big sister waiting in the parking lot. I didn't know what to do, but my aunt told me to give them a big hug and a kiss. It felt awkward. We went to North Hoover Street. It was a five-bedroom house with one bathroom for eleven people. We had a backyard, a front yard, a garden, and a carport. Eventually the awkwardness went away. I felt comfortable and thought we were going to live there forever. It was the perfect place, even though it was chaotic.

I had a dysfunctional family, but I will always remember holidays and the daily routines. On Christmas and New Year's Day, my grandma made her delicious traditional recipes. She and my grandpa threw coins every New Year's Eve when the clock struck twelve. For eight years we would to go to church every Sunday, and my grandma cooked us breakfast, lunch, and dinner. Then one day we received a notice from our landlord stating, "Must move in 60 days." It was devastating. I wanted to cry. We looked for a place, but it was difficult to find a house where we could all fit. We went our separate ways.

My parents, sister, and I moved in with my mom's brother in Burbank. The neighborhood was clean, rich, and quiet. My uncle has a nice two-bedroom house with two bathrooms, two living rooms, a kitchen, and a garage. Living in Burbank felt like prison. My sister and I weren't allowed to go out without permission. It was different from the busier but less lonesome LA.

Two months later my mother found a place back in LA on La Mirada Avenue. It was nice going back because I felt more alive and free. We live in a one-bedroom apartment without Internet, beds, cable, or a home phone, but we have a computer, cell phones, and a television. We don't have beds because we prefer the floor.

The saddest part of the way we are living is that no one's home and we don't communicate as well as before. Stacks of boxes divide the living room. Everyone just works, eats, and sleeps. Even holidays don't seem like holidays. Most of the time I don't want to be home because I get depressed; now I spend most of my time with my boyfriend.

Moving from the Philippines to California is still changing my life.

Nerijus Ramanauskas

HOME SWEET HOME

My story is one of a life turned upside down. Now, I know this happens to many, but nevertheless each case is dramatic to whomever it befalls. In my particular case, it was when faith and destiny dreamed up the cruelest nightmare for this inexperienced youth. At just eleven years of age, these forces took my life away and pressed upon me to start anew.

I remember those days in Lithuania when nothing bothered me. I enjoyed my childhood just as much any other kid. Each day was a paradise, with sun in my face and sand beneath my toes. Life seemed to be its own reward then, but everything changed when my father came home with a letter one day. He announced we were moving to America. For my brother, who is four years older than I am, the news was a blessing. But, to me, it was a shock. It meant I would have to say good-bye to my friends, my home, and everything I had come to love.

As I was leaving the port, it was heartbreaking to look back. It seemed the sun hid beneath the clouds, and the soft sand turned to coarse stone. Even though I was sad to think of the possibility of never seeing my cousins, I knew that I was fortunate: I had a supportive family at my side that cheered and helped me all the way through.

In February 2002, we arrived in California. While it wasn't physically a hard trip, the burden was emotionally heavy. The next years weren't the easiest in my life, and it was hard to adjust—remembering all you've left behind is hard. I've noticed I have become a different person here. Because my parents did not speak English, a lot of their troubles have fallen on my shoulders. Paperwork, social security problems, and everyday questions depended on my answers. I had to assist them in daily problems I never faced before, which hardened my character, bolstered my resolve, and made me more independent in the process. In the long run, life here made me face a lot of my fears and challenged my ways of thinking. As I sit here writing and reflecting upon the move, I realize it all turned out for the best.

Slowly, but surely, the sun again seems to be coming out of a gloomy mist to brighten my day, and the road ahead appears to be covered in sandy hills as I push through the daily clutter of troubles. I found an interest I hope will become a prosperous career one day—graphic design—which would not have been a possibility back in Lithuania. I've found many new friends here in Los Angeles. And, as the old memories fade from my mind, I have come to accept this opportunity-filled land.

I left a part of me on the other side of the globe, with my homeland and old life. Even though I still communicate with my cousins back home, the nostalgia of it is rapidly being replaced with the new and wonderful experiences I am encountering here. America is becoming my new "home, sweet home."

Narek Avetisian

MY LANGUAGE OF CLOSENESS

My language of closeness is Armenian. I was born and raised in Armenia until I was six years old. I came from Armenia with my mom and dad in 1997. We did not understand a word of English. I felt like an outsider.

I went to first grade at Los Feliz Elementary School. The teacher tried so hard to teach me English, but it was almost impossible for me to learn. The first word I learned was *hi*. Five months after my first day of school I learned the numbers one to one thousand. I had private tutoring classes to help me learn my numbers and the alphabet because they were extremely difficult. After about a year, I learned how to say sentences. By fifth grade I spoke English with no problem at all, but I still had an accent. I became fluent in sixth grade.

In seventh grade I went to Armenia for two months to see my relatives. It was very hard for me to speak fluent Armenian. Because I spoke so much English, I forgot my own language. That wasn't a big deal because my relatives retaught me how to speak fluently. After two months, I returned to America and had forgotten how to speak English. But it wasn't long before I became fluent again.

Before going to Armenia, I didn't have that many friends. When I came back, I made a lot of friends at King Middle School, but people made fun of my accent. I tried and tried to get rid of my accent and finally, in ninth grade, I did.

I went back to Armenia at the end of ninth grade for four months. My family was thinking about not returning to America because we missed our relatives too much. I really wanted to stay in my home country because I was born there, and also because it is very beautiful. But if we stayed in Armenia for more than four months, I would probably forget English again. We decided to come back at the beginning of the third month.

Learning English is like a roller coaster, because when the roller coaster goes up I learn English, but then when it goes down I forget. Now, I am in a low grade, and I am thinking about going back to Armenia because I am starting to miss my relatives again. Sometimes, when I talk to my relatives in Armenia by phone, I tell them how much English I have learned and how much I like the language.

It was very hard for me to learn two languages. If you stay in a country that only speaks one language, you forget the other language. I went through a lot of stress throughout my life because I didn't know the language and because I couldn't get good grades. I went through all that emotion to get to where I am today. Now, I am fluent in both English and Armenian.

Vahe Halajyan

LIFE AND BASKETBALL

When I first came to America, the only sport that I knew about was soccer. About a year after I came to America, I started playing basketball. I was horrible. At the time I did not like to play; I just liked to watch it on TV. I watched the Los Angeles Lakers the most because their games were on a local channel and I didn't have cable.

I started to watch every single game they played, and they became my favorite basketball team. They had the "big two" combination of the best players—Kobe Bryant and Shaquille O'Neal. This amazing combination was—and still is—the best combination in NBA history. Shaq was the best center in the NBA, and Kobe, though very young, was still one of the best players in the league. During the first two years that I watched the Lakers, they won two NBA titles. They were the best team in the NBA.

I always watched their games and kept track of their statistics on NBA.com. If I could not watch a game, I would look at the score on the website. Watching the Lakers made we want to play basketball more. I began to love the sport—both watching it and playing it. I got more into it and started to play it every day at school. There were many kids who were better than me, but that still did not stop me.

I practiced every day and got better and better at it.

Now, I am part of a basketball program called AEBC. Since I started playing basketball, it has become my favorite sport and I don't regret learning how to play.

Yesenia Gonzalez

SOCCER

It was September, and I wanted to be on a team. My best friend Kimberly told me there would be soccer tryouts the next day, and she asked me if I wanted to go with her. I said I would think about it.

"Please, I want to be on the soccer team with you," she begged.

"OK, I will go with you to tryouts tomorrow," I said.

I didn't really care about soccer; I just wanted to be on a team.

The next day, I was nervous because I had never played soccer. When the bell rang after sixth period, Kimberly and I went to the girls' locker room to change. To make it worse, I had the wrong shoes—flat Vans. All the other girls had running shoes.

Once we got dressed, we left the locker rooms and went to the bleachers to meet with the coach. We went up to him and handed her our emergency cards. There were about forty girls trying out, and I got nervous because they looked like they'd played soccer before. We had a feeling we weren't going to make the team.

When Coach Reyes finished collecting the emergency cards, we walked to the field and then ran around it twice. Once we finished running, we stretched, and then we practiced with the ball. We got in rows of eight and dribbled the ball. Jackie, my friend since elementary school, helped me out because she had been playing soccer since she was five. Jackie told me I was doing well, but once the other coach, Coach Hernandez, looked at me, I kicked the ball too far because I got nervous. Jackie started to laugh at me, and I started to laugh, too.

"Do you think we will make it onto the team?" I asked Kimberly after tryouts.

"I don't know," she said.

Two weeks passed before Ms. Gedemer summoned me to her office. Once I walked in, she said, "Congratulations!"

"For what?" I asked.

"You made the soccer team," she said.

I was so happy!

"Good luck," she said, as I walked out of her room.

I was excited as I walked to my second period class. When I got inside the classroom, I couldn't wait to tell Kimberly. I looked at the clock, and there were only twenty minutes until the bell rang for nutrition. Once the bell rang, Kimberly was already there.

"Guess what?" she said.

"What?" I replied.

"I made it on the soccer team!" Kimberly said.

"Me, too!"

When practice began, we were nervous because we knew some of the girls had already been playing soccer, and we thought they might judge us. But it wasn't like that. When we were practicing with the ball, they helped us and the other girls out.

Two months passed, and then Coach Reyes told me I couldn't be on the team anymore because I didn't have the grades. I wanted to cry. I'd been putting all my effort to get better at it for nothing. Coach Reyes told me that if I raised my grades by next semester, I could get back on the team. The next day at school, I did all my work in class to raise my grades.

My parents never found out there was a time when I wasn't on the team. I decided not to tell them because my mom paid one hundred dollars for my uniform. They would have gotten mad if I told them I wasn't on the team, but I learned my lesson even though my parents never knew.

When the next semester started, I had already raised my grades. It was a Monday when I went to Coach Reyes' classroom to ask her if I could get back on the team.

"Did you raise your grades?"

"Yes."

She told me I could start the next day.

Ever since that day, I've kept my grades up to stay in soccer. Soccer has changed my way of being, because before I wouldn't have cared about my grades as much as I do now. If I don't have good grades, I can't be on the soccer team. Soccer has been a place for me to be happy when I'm feeling down.

Eduardo Ponce de Leon

LEARNING FROM MY PAST

When I was little, my life was different because I lived in Mexico City where the people were calmer, friendlier, and more trustworthy. There were some mean people as well, though: greedy and selfish people. When I was about seven years old, my life was happy and sad at the same time because the mean people used to bother me all the time, trying to hit me and take my money away. Those people were jealous because I had money most of the time. They tried to take my money, but I wouldn't let them. So they would beat me up and make me cry. The teenagers who lived near my house were scarier because they would just beat me up for any reason. I couldn't say anything because they would hit me again. That's how my childhood was: I was always getting threatened.

One day I told my mom about the guy that hit me the most. My uncle was there when I told her, and he asked me why I hadn't told anybody. I said I was scared. My uncle went the next day and told the guy, "You better stop messing with my nephew and hitting him, or else I'll do the same thing to you." What my uncle did was really kind. He took care of me while my dad was in Los Angeles. The guy stopped bothering me as well, so I was happy afterwards—I could hang around with my friends without worrying about people hitting me.

In elementary school in Mexico City, I was one of the best students in class, and in sports as well. One of my favorite sports was soccer, but I also played football, basketball, and tennis. I received scholarships for English and computer classes. When I was almost eleven years old, my mom told me we were going to go to Los Angeles with my dad. I asked when, but my mom didn't answer me.

"But, Mom, what about my education right here and my scholarships?" I said.

"Don't worry," my mom answered. "Over there you're going to study as well, but in another language."

"But I like being here with everybody and our family," I said.

"Don't worry. You'll get used to it over there," my mom said.

I said, "OK, then." I was happy because I was going to see my dad—I hadn't seen him for the longest time. But when the day came, I was kind of sad because I was leaving the people I loved.

"Don't worry," my mom said. "It's a good thing for you to go to Los Angeles because in the United States they give a lot of opportunities to children."

When we arrived in Los Angeles, I was really excited about seeing my dad. He is the greatest, because he will always love you and take care of you and give you everything you want, just to see you happy. As time went on, I was trying my best to get good grades in school, but there was a problem—the friends I had were trouble-makers. I was being influenced by them, and I started acting like them. My mom realized how I was changing, and she told me one day we needed to talk seriously.

"Remember what I told you before we came to this country?" she asked.

"Yes," I answered. "They give you a lot of opportunities."

Then she asked why I wasn't taking advantage of them, and I said I didn't know. She said that in this life, we have one chance, and I wasn't taking advantage of it.

"I'm sorry, Mom. I'll try," I said.

"You better, son."

By the seventh grade, I started thinking about why I came to this country. Here, there are gang problems, drugs, and sexual abuse. I think I was safer in my country. I said to myself that I didn't want to get killed here just because some people don't like me. But at the same time, this is a country that gives you the opportunity to open the door to a great future. Some people who come from other countries don't take advantage of this, so I started caring less about the people around me—even though some of them were my friends. As my English got better, I started getting better grades at school, too. So now I just try harder in school and do my best so I can go to college and study for a career I like.

Matthew Kongthong

LEARNING TO LIVE MY FUTURE

My life has its ups and downs like everyone else's. I remember my good times and my bad. I'm growing up every day, day by day, one step toward the future. I don't know how my life is going to be in the future. I'm sure a lot of teenagers my age don't know yet. If I could relive my childhood, I would, because when you're a kid you don't even know how much fun you're having. As you mature, you start to understand how life is. Once you're in high school, you have to start thinking of your future, and it seems like there's very little time.

Some people say, "You only live once. You're gonna die one day, so why not live for the moment? Live life before it's gone. Why think about your future?" My mother told me, "The only person who decides your fate is you." It's true that you only have one life, and that you should live life, but if you just live life, where can it get you? Life isn't fair or perfect. You can live life, but it doesn't mean that you will have a better life. When you're in school, you hang out with your friends and have fun. But school is also for education, and education can get you somewhere. I didn't realize that until high school. If I don't do well in school, then how will I go to college? If I don't go to college, how will I get a good job to support myself? That's why I understand that I had my fun when I was a kid. I just didn't realize it until now.

Every day when I go home, I look at my mom and see how hard it is for her to support two kids. My mom didn't have the same childhood I did. At the age of fourteen, she had to wake up early in the morning and sell food just to support her family. At the age of fifteen, she had to drop out of school because her mother didn't have the money. When she was twenty-five, she moved to America so she could make money to send back to her family. She attempted to finish school, but couldn't. My mom always told me I have a better childhood than she did, and that I can have a better life if I get a good education. When I think about my mom's childhood and compare it to mine, I think of all the chances I have to get a free education. Many of us have free education, but choose not to use it. Some countries don't have free education. Some of these people don't have a good life because they don't have money and a chance to get an education. If we all had free education, we would have a better life. As a child, you don't know how precious life is. You don't know any better because you are just a kid. As we grow up, we learn more. My mom tried to tell me this when I was younger, but I never listened.

Now, I understand. I have two years left until I graduate from high school. I have two years to think about my future. Everyone has a chance for a good future. Some decide to just live their life and spend it all with friends, and some decide to do well in school. Some do both. The point to life is to live it, of course, but to make life better, we must be doing something that can get us somewhere. You can still live life and do well in school. You can't make a life by just spending time with your friends.

No one can decide my fate but me. I had my chance to live life, and I did. In the future, I'll remember the good times I had as a child, but now it's time for me to do something that can make my life better.

John Rosales

SPOTS UNDERNEATH MY EYELIDS

I guess I have been going through what you call "depression." I've been so immersed within myself I've just begun to notice the effects of my actions. Everything has been in vain so far, and it seems like there really is no light at the end of the tunnel. It's only been recently that I've actually been pondering everything and the reasons why we do things. The importance of something, really, is just that "it's something to do." It all really does end the same, so what does it matter?

This existence is one of toil and suffering, one where no matter how good you are there is always someone better, and there is always that one thing that makes your perfect day a complete disaster. It doesn't even matter who you are because we are nothing in this world. We are just ordinary people, and in history it is not the ordinary people who are remembered, but the person who was important, that person who shaped the people. If you are not that one person, then all you really are is an extra in the background, just as replaceable to the world as the person next to you.

I guess I've come to grips with how life really is to me. So far it has just been a pattern that I have never really broken out of. So far it's been good, bad, worse, and finally indifferent. The best example of this was when I once had the most amazing day: everything was finally going my way. The next day, it just somehow went away, and only one thought did that. I was about eight years old at the time, and I saw a movie at home with my father. At the end of it I just simply thought about what death was like. Like a cold rush of water, it filled me with dread for what really does come after this. I felt like coming to tears and not wanting this to end, but I forgot

51

about it only one hour later, and it's been like this ever since. I've tried to come to grips with my mortality, but so far it's only been in vain.

I've been told why I have to do things, but I always think in the back of my mind, *So what? Tomorrow will be tomorrow and this day will be nothing a year from now.* This may explain why I've been more or less a procrastinator. I tend to analyze things because of my mentality on "importance," just a word for something to do for the hell of it. Because there is always something "important" coming up, it never seems like anything really is important. That "important" homework assignment is "important" to your grade, not mine. What really makes it "important" then? It only matters to you, not to me, and not to the world.

I spend the majority of my time thinking while listening to a certain song on repeat for a few hours. These songs usually help express these ideas and form words that my mind knows, but my mouth cannot say. These ideas I only share with myself because no one can ever really understand someone's ideas. That person can only apply another's thoughts to their own life and assume it refers to them.

I haven't really let this ideology consume me. I've found that not thinking about it tends to help suppress it. I've tried to surround myself with music and emotions that, at the very least, help shield my true state from everyone around me. It helps avoid the constant stares and typical barrage of questions about why I act the way I do. The answer is easy: I think far too much and do very little about anything. You spend time doing things, while thinking feels like an eternity. So if I just spend my time thinking, then I never get anywhere, but at the same time I'm right where I want to be: the place I love to call the spot. It is a feeling more than an actual place; it's a free white zone where I can think about anything and feel whatever I prefer according to my mood. Music enhances this, and emotions stimulate it.

This stimulation usually results in a freaked-out version of me where I am very happy, depressed, or enraged. It is truly a wonderful state in which I can get some very progressive thoughts out. An example of such a thought would be why chocolate pudding, when frozen, does not produce chocolate ice cream. This may seem rather stupid, but it is my bliss in that I can freely think about anything, no matter how stupid it may seem. I know that it is trivial, but it helps soothe things that are better kept under wraps. These feelings that I keep suppressed are what may be keeping me from fully being all that I can be, but I myself am a lazy slob and would much rather think about something else than go out and make a change .

The one thing I have noticed, though, is my continued want for things I cannot or do not wish to have. It seems rather contradictory, but it makes sense in a way. I am at peace with what I have, but I want more. I do not want more, because what I have now is enough. What I can have I do not choose to go after because I know I can have it at any time I want. What I cannot have I do go for because I shall never have it and let myself believe that I cannot even though I know that is a lie. These thoughts result in many contradictions for me, because what at one point was good is sour and what was bad is now a friend. Love means hate, and to me, frankly, hate is far more fun to toy with than adoration. For this reason I seek to be hated; love, in my opinion, is for the weak, for it clouds one's mind and makes one a shell of oneself. I am a bit of a masochist in thinking so because my thoughts are what help me sustain this idea. It is my metal lunchbox, and with it I'm armed really well so that the big bully won't stick his finger in my chest.

Unlike most cases of depression in teenagers though, I make fun of it. In doing so it isn't as bleak, because fear means nothing when you have a lunchbox, pain is just a word unless you think it hurts, and emotions make a really good excuse for anything if you are around simpletons who honestly believe emotions control you. I try to take advantage of myself the way I do with others. I put myself in situations where I have many options but very few right ones. In doing so, I have the illusion of "choice," but in reality for me there is no "choice" by "regular" people's standards, so I call it two ideas: one self-destructive, one constructive. I'll gladly choose any just for the fact that it is something for me to do. After all, I have nothing but time to kill with me, myself, and I.

For me, the demons in my head are just dreams wrapped in nightmares, and once I come to grips with that I can start to function right.

Catherine Hugo

THE FIRST THING TO ME

When I was in my hometown, I used to go to church every Sunday with my parents and other relatives. We used to pray together and, after church, eat together. When I moved to America, things changed.

I don't have many relatives, and not all of my family was able to move here. It's sad to think you left people you love, but that's how life goes. You are not always going to be happy with every decision you make.

Time goes by, and I must accept I have to be away from those I love. It's hard for me to be away from them because they're my family, and I love them. As I reminisce about the past, I make a goal for myself, a goal I know the people I left behind will be proud of: to have good grades in school and to have a nice future. Little by little, I am trying to reach these goals. Every day, I go to school. I also have a part-time job, so I don't have to ask my parents for money. I know they're already paying for a lot of things. I told them that even though I am young, I want to experience the things I will encounter when I grow up so I will be ready.

As I go about my everyday life I hardly pray, and I haven't had much time to go to Mass every Sunday—this makes me feel sad. It feels like I have forgotten the life I used to have. I don't have much time to communicate with my relatives because I have been busy.

I tried to get back the closeness I used to have with my family, but it seems like things aren't working. I tried to figure out why, and there is this one thing that came to mind—praying. *Maybe this is the reason why my life is incomplete,* I thought. *I haven't had enough time to pray to God.* Even though I know I have been missing Sunday Mass, I just ignored it and got on with my plans. Now, I know praying shouldn't be ignored, because it is important to me; therefore, I started my life again by praying, which helps me a lot. Since then, I have started to accomplish my goals—which makes me feel proud.

I was feeling happy about everything until I heard that my grandfather died. I acted crazy and couldn't believe that I was not going to see him again in life. No matter how much I wanted him back I couldn't do anything. All I did was pray, hoping that he's happy now. While I pray it feels like I am talking to my grandfather. Now praying is always the first thing to me.

Abraham Betancourt

AM I SUCH A DREAMER?

The beginning of life—the beginning of *my* life—began six months ago. That was when I alienated myself from everyone. I felt it was time to put myself in a room, a room that would become my only world. The real world would just be a place in which my world would test itself. I wonder: how long will I stay here? The question is: why sit in a room for such a long time? I ask myself that every day. I don't have the answer yet, but I hope I will soon. My friends and others, who know that I spend most of my time in my room, wonder about it, but never ask. Soon they won't have to know the answer, but just what happened in that room.

As a kid, I was never social. I spent most of my time just watching the other little boys and girls live their lives while I stood on the sidelines. It made me happy, so I never thought of it as a bad thing. For seven years, I did this and never wondered about it, but others did. They would ask, "Are you crazy or something?" I still remember some of those faces and laugh, because I have become more social but still get the same question.

When entering middle school, I knew things would change in a major way but never thought they would lead me from my normal position. The beginning of sixth grade was normal: I was quiet and not very social. My seventh-grade and eighth-grade years changed me; I met some people whom I thought were good, but soon found out they weren't. I remained quiet and antisocial in middle school.

Then came John Marshall High School, the one place I think of as mind-changing and full of surprises. My freshman year was no different than the previous years; I was isolated from people and constantly doing work for school activities. Sophomore year was a bit different because I met some new people and discovered people's weakness for unconditional love and their obsessions with people whom they've had sex with, although I personally don't consider this love. In the summer of my sophomore year, I was faced with problems of understanding why certain things happen in their particular way. This involved a lot of people's mentalities and the way they strive for something more. After watching my own mind fall apart, I decided just to sit in my room and think until I encountered something I never had before. This became addicting to me, and I spent most of my time writing music and composing it in a style that I hadn't heard before. I have many tracks hidden, written in a way that only I can read.

Society affected my thinking. I observed and analyzed things that bothered me. I watched things disappear without change, then I would return to my room and figure these things out. My composing helped me with my thinking process. I consider my room a good place. If it was just an isolated area in some forest I would sit and watch it burn just to erase all of my memories. I don't alienate myself from others for bad reasons; it's just who I am, and it's a habit for me. I love people and envy them, but I have seen too much and others haven't seen enough.

Up until today, February 12, 2007, I remain in my room. It's fun sitting, thinking, writing music, and then listening to it. Some of my friends try to get me out more, but I always return to my room. I should be more outgoing. Who knows—I'll see how far I get. I never gave myself a good reason for being in my room, but every day I felt as if I was just taken away from reality. I thought there was no way out, but later I began to feel that I would stay home forever. Maybe one day, when I finally see the perfect day, nothing else will matter. That day will be the most perfect day that I've ever seen. For now, I don't know what everyone is coming to. Everything is all wrong and all right. All these things wear me out and make me feel a lot like a broken man who will just crumble and burn.

Dixey Hernandez

THE STEREO TYPE

Ever since I was a kid I've loved music. When I was about four or five, I can remember my mom buying me black, shiny shoes with small heels. I twirled around like crazy in those little things to Selena. I could still remember the way I would get dizzy, dancing to the *Cumbia* beats and listening to her beautiful and elegant voice. I felt close to my culture when I heard the sounds of romantic Spanish words and saw dance movements that were as unexplainable as they were unbelievably amazing. My life revolved around the Latin music culture, and everything felt full of joy. Everything felt so put together. It was a kind of life that had no worries. I wasn't a person to be judged. It was a life that I don't think I could go back to. As I grew up my music taste evolved as well as others' perception of me.

After I turned seven, I stopped showing interest in Latin music or dancing. My love for it had gone away because my choices expanded. Music in English came along: mainstream pop, rap, and R & B. It was everywhere. It was the cool thing to listen to, and it made you want to sing along and learn the choreographed dance moves. In middle school, as I made new friends, I met different kinds of people. I saw more kids who were into the rock genres. It was not until then that I figured out that a person is defined by not only their physical appearance but also by their musical taste. When I would look at them, I shivered and said, "I will never turn into one of them." I thought they were rebels who destroyed things or outcasts who didn't have friends. I was categorizing people by musical taste as well as getting criticized myself. At eleven I got sick and tired of music talking so excessively about women, guns, and money. I didn't want to be a girl who would end up with guys who dropped out of school or got pregnant—the things the rap genre explored. The thug life didn't seem like much of a choice. The reason why I liked it so much was because it was in style and everyone else did, but I wasn't everyone else. Thinking back, I was a very judgmental and stereotypical person.

Now my life consists of heavy metal and some alternative rock music like Avenged Sevenfold, Bullet for My Valentine, and It Dies Today. I am what I once feared as a child, but I'm happy. I realized that you don't have to dress scary and dark to enjoy rock. I remember going to my first concert to see Simple Plan. It was then and there where I really fell in love with music, not because it was in, but because I had fun. When you walk into a show, you can feel the body heat of people coming together just waiting for the band to come on stage. I love hearing the music through my heart as it beats faster and faster when the band starts to play. I love the cheering and chanting for the band as if they are glorious, and raising our hands to try to reach out for them. When it all comes to an end you have so much adrenaline you feel like you could keep on going. Then, waking in the morning sore from the pushing and accidental hits that you didn't feel from the night before—it's amazing.

There are thick borders between people because of the music they like. Almost everyone in school has their own clique in which they all dress similarly and share the same musical interests. People will always be judged by their appearance and interests. They will likely give a simple stare and think *they're not like me* and keep on walking. Even my parents say that rock is the "devil's music," which always makes me laugh. Now I stand in the same spotlight of judgment, being labeled a lot of things because of the way I dress or the music I listen to, but I have learned to ignore other people's opinions. With music, I can be proud to say I don't do it to fit a crowd or do the cool thing. I do it for me. I know that as I get older my taste is going to change. I found my spot in life as someone who can be labeled but doesn't care because she found what she likes best. Bill Cosby summed it up when he said, "Nothing separates the generations more than music. By the time a child is eight or nine, he has developed a passion for his own music that is even stronger than his passions for procrastination and weird clothes." My life has a soundtrack, and it's very different from anybody else's, and I am proud of that.

Paulina Perez

COME AS YOU ARE

Kurt Cobain is my Idol. I first heard him when I was seven years old and my dad would play Nirvana's *In Utero* album. His music eventually got stuck in my head. When I get depressed, I listen to his songs. His lyrics say what people feel before they even know they feel it. When I listen to Nirvana, it's a feeling I can't explain. His writing makes you think he really knows how life is, and he can express it in a song and make people feel better. He is probably the best songwriter there has ever been.

Nirvana's "Heart-Shaped Box" reminds me of a time when I was mad at my mom. When I would try to explain something to her, she would think I was wrong or dumb. *She eyes me like a Pisces when I am weak,* the song says.

This one time, she made fun of me because I said my hearing doesn't work that well, and she tried to insult me by saying, "You don't have any of your four senses, anyway." I told her we don't have four senses; we have five. She got mad and told me some other stuff, made me feel bad. So I went to my room. *I've been locked inside your heart-shaped box for weeks.*

Kurt Cobain and I have the same perspective on the world and about bands. In his journals, he wrote things I think are true. In one of his journals, he wrote that all thirteen-year-old prepubescent kids hate their parents and feel weird around the opposite sex. When I was that age, I hated my parents because they didn't notice I was growing up and treated me like a little kid. I also felt weird around the opposite sex. When I was younger, my second grade teacher made us sit in assigned seats. My classmates would think it was weird we had to sit next to boys because the girls said they had cooties.

Back in middle school, Kurt also inspired my friends and me to learn to play the guitar and bass. I liked the beat and the guitar sound. After school, we went to a free guitar class and tried to play "Smells like Teen Spirit." We liked the intro, and it seemed easy to play and sing along to. The intro went, *Load up on guns, bring your friends, it's fun to lose and to pretend. She's over-bored and self-assured; oh no I know a dirty word.* We played in groups, and it was funny when someone tried to play the solo and messed up. They either played the wrong note, or they tried to make up new ones as they played along. We all got better, so we tried to play the guitar and sing at the same time, but someone would mess up the lyrics, and we would laugh. Then, the teacher would get mad because we weren't practicing what we were supposed to, and we would get in trouble.

Even though Kurt Cobain is dead, he is still a big part of my life. He still brings joy to me when I listen to his lyrics, and he brings back good memories I will cherish forever. He helped me feel better in depressing times, and he inspired me to play my guitar and bass. I thank my dad for playing that Nirvana cassette when I was seven, because if he hadn't, Nirvana's music would have never gotten stuck in my head.

Come as you are, as you were, as I want you to be. As a friend, as a friend, as a known memory.

Roque Ek

LIFE AND ITS TRIPS

Life has many overwhelming experiences. Some change your personality; others traumatize you for the rest of your natural life. February 1, 1991, was the day my sister's mother brought me into this hellhole we call Earth. We lived in Northridge for a while, about two years. Then that earthquake happened and we skedaddled to Panorama City. That's where I almost died.

It's a crazy story. I was about two years old, and my mother was washing some clothes. There was a pool right next to the laundromat, and my mother was so busy with the clothes that she set me down and I wandered off. All I remember now is my mom pulling me out of the pool. That experience made me think about how my parents were raising me.

Then came the thug years. First grade through fourth are a total blank. Memory loss is another side effect of harsh reality. D.A.R.E., a program that was supposed to prevent us from using drugs, came in fifth grade. Well, this program messed me up. Instead of preventing me from using drugs, it made me want to experience them. Drugs aren't the answer to most things, but they aren't a bad thing either; it depends on the user and the drug. Drugs lead you to things you don't want to do, but sometimes they lead you to a happier life. By this age, I knew what was up. I had seen very crazy stuff happen on my block. Once I saw one of the neighbor kids get jacked for his shoes. All of this at age eleven!

I guess I knew about the streets and how they work. You pick things up as you begin to hang out. The thug life never interested me back then. There are people who try to help you; I consider them friends. But there are people who pull you into their world. You learn too much from these people. I consider them homies, people

62

who are down for whatever you're down for. I have had people who changed my life completely, and I know that I have changed people's lives. My parents have a great deal to do with how I act now. School changed me a lot; at an early age it taught me some things I didn't want to know. The surroundings in my neighborhood influence the things that I do now.

I started liking graffiti art in the sixth grade, thanks to my friend. Art is a big part of my life because I can express the way I feel in colors and shapes. Graffiti art can sometimes become your figure. For example, there are very well-paid graffiti artists from LA like Crol, Marka47, Man One, and Pose2. Even if some people don't agree, I think graffiti is a way of life. The government took cracking down on graffiti to another level, making it a crime now. This makes me mad because artists are in jail for what they believe. Whatever happened to freedom of speech? When it comes to living by the rules, it is sometimes better to break them. By following what you believe you can achieve basically anything. I have met people whom I still know, and people I hate, thanks to graffiti and the stupid stuff I do. Stuff happens in life that we do not expect, and with those last words I leave you to ponder some of the things I have just said. Peace.

Dennis Coto

A BLOODY NOSE SERENADE

Change is a difficult thing that we all face. Change can bring good things and bad things. Change can happen quickly or slowly-but-surely. During the fifteen years of my life, I've faced many changes. I was born in El Salvador, but I was brought to the US when I was eight months old. I don't know anything about my country; I've only heard about it and seen a couple of pictures. Sometimes I wish I knew more. Ugh. I hate my life; it's always been a big mess. Well, not always...

When I was in elementary school, I was really smart. I got straight A's. I didn't get in trouble until third grade, when I threw rocks at people. Afterwards, I didn't get in trouble again; I pretty much learned my lesson. Kindergarten through fourth grade were my favorite years, but a big change awaited me...

Fifth grade was OK. I didn't get into trouble; I didn't do anything great either. After I finished fifth grade, I was supposed to go to Lacumbre Middle School, but I had to move. It was all very fast, like a punch in the face, a punch that leaves your nose bloody and broken. It hurt.

We lived in Santa Barbara. The rent was really high, so we moved to Los Angeles. My three sisters and I didn't like it one bit, but we had no say in this. I think we all hated that we had to leave our home. I lost so many friends when we left Santa Barbara. I knew I probably wasn't ever going to see them again, and if I did, they probably wouldn't remember me. I didn't have anywhere to live here, so I lived with my aunt for about four months. I wasn't going to school because my grades got lost during the move. I had to wait for my old school to send copies. While I waited for my grades to come, I made some friends here, but I guess they weren't the best influence on me. (We're good friends, though.)

Anyway, when I got my grades, I had to attend Thomas Starr King Middle School. I didn't like it there because we had to wear uniforms and I thought uniforms were lame. (I hate when people wear the same thing I do, ha-ha.) I didn't really fit in, and I felt a bit odd. I didn't know anyone there, and back then I was still nice (not anymore!); everyone picked on me. I hated when I was polite to people and they were just completely rude. I grew bitter and lazy. I didn't do my work, I lost my interest in school, and my grades started slipping. My teachers grew worried about my grades and my participation in class, but I didn't care. I was a lost cause to some, but I still didn't care. I failed a lot of my classes, and I didn't have a care in the world.

Then came high school, and when I walked through those doors I thought to myself, *Dennis! You really screwed up in middle school; don't mess up here!* To my dismay, I'm still doing the same stuff I did in middle school: fooling around, not doing my work, and not paying attention. And my life has never been as chaotic as it is now.

Some things never change, but I wish I would. I've got many problems right now: I'm missing a lot of my credits, I have some family problems, and I feel really insecure about myself. My life is a mess, and I wish it wouldn't be. But then again, I'm the only one who can really change that.

Isaac Hernandez

GETTING OUT OF THE GAME

I started to see the real world when I turned eight. I began noticing all the corruption in the streets and found out what drugs were. I would be walking down the street or driving with my mom, noticing people dealing and doing drugs. It was not a pretty sight. Life was getting interesting, but more dangerous.

The first time I had a gun pointed at me was when I was nine.

I thought to myself, *Am I going to die?*

Is he going to steal from me?

Why is he pointing a gun at me?

What did I ever do wrong? ·

I was furious. If I had a gun, I would have used it.

When I got home, I didn't want to say anything to my parents, because I knew my mom would freak. After that day, I didn't go outside for weeks. I would stay in my house playing video games, and that was basically it. I was scared.

I entered middle school when I was twelve, and that's when everything changed. My friends started becoming gangsters, and everything was just going wrong for me. I tried not doing any bad stuff, yet I did lots of things I regret to this day. I regret being a tagger. The first time they gave me a name, I felt as if I had done something great, but now I realize it was a complete waste of time. I didn't win anything by tagging; all I won was a beating from other kids a few months later.

I was in the seventh grade the first time a friend was killed in a drive-by shooting. That made me think about what I was doing. I wondered if I was going to end up dead. So, after that day, I stopped doing all those horrible things. I would still say hello to my old friends, but as years went by, one would always end up becoming lost. Playing games kept me out of trouble. I did that a lot because it was the only thing to keep me away from the bad stuff.

I started picking myself up in eighth grade. I tried not doing anything bad, yet I got peer-pressured into ditching a couple of times. But, for a few months, I managed to stay out of trouble on the streets and in school. One year passed, and I was ready to go to high school. I was excited. But, a week before ninth grade, I saw my mom's friend's son die in front of me. He was riding a bike and got shot six times in the chest. The shooter walked up to him while he bled to death on the ground, and, seconds later, I heard another shot. That was the finishing shot. When I saw that last bullet go into his chest, I panicked. My mouth went from wet to suddenly dry, and I couldn't feel my body. My brain kept sending messages to my body to take cover, but my body didn't respond. I just stood there on the porch. When I walked to the body, and saw him choking on his own blood, trying to gasp for air, I knew I would end up like that if I continued being a tagger and doing other things. This really affected the way I thought about gangs, crews, and so on.

Finally, I had entered ninth grade. I became interested in my studies and paid less attention to the streets. But, as days passed, it began to feel the same as middle school—the only difference was we didn't have to wear uniforms. Then, I made a new friend. All we would do was hacky sack, play games, and graphic design. It was fun; I guess that was my way out of trouble.

A year went by, and it was time to enter tenth grade. I thought it was going to be just another year. The AP classes were fun, but difficult, and I regret being lazy because I failed, and I wanted to really try in my second semester.

These are my secrets.

Well, some of them.

Dre

GROWING UP WITH DISTRACTIONS

My younger years of life were innocent. My parents loved my siblings and me; they cared about us and kept us happy. They had support from my grandparents, who are very religious people. They would take my siblings and me to church every Sunday, just like all religious Filipino grandparents. My father wasn't always around because he worked two jobs almost every day, so my grandfather was my father figure. He took care of me for the first four years of my life: feeding me, washing me, and watching me. But I didn't know that he smoked for nearly forty years. So, on December 24, 1995, he passed away. When I went to his funeral, I was too young to understand. All I remember is him lying in the coffin.

After my grandfather's death, I began absorbing and learning how to act the right way, understanding what was right and what was wrong. I was turning into a "good boy." When I went to school, I received very good comments and grades from my kindergarten teacher. That was pretty much the case from then to the fifth grade.

In sixth grade, though, I began seeing what could happen to students if they didn't grow up like I did. Months later, I gave in and began slacking off: not doing my homework and schoolwork. After that month of slacking off, my progress report came out, and my parents saw a big fat D. After that, my parents were really mad—I could tell because they took away my toys and games until my next progress report came out, which was about a month later. During that month, I thought of the things I could have done to prevent what happened to me, like doing all my schoolwork and homework. I returned to my smarter ways and improved on my studies—all because I got a single D.

In the seventh grade, I did very well, the same as always. But during that time, my family and I started to realize what my father had been doing for roughly four years: he was on crystal meth. We noticed he was short-tempered and acted like a jerk. He was also very awake and active. All of my mother's and father's closest friends were very surprised. My father is a smart and nice man, and all of my parents' friends would strongly agree. He was the kindest person ever in my life. But, months after we found out, he suddenly became mean and confused about everything. Because he acted like this, my grandmother felt that he endangered my mother and siblings, and she had to kick him out. When he still lived with us, we were all scared of being in the house with him because he had a bad temper and, if we got on his bad side, he would just yell for no reason. My mother was even afraid of asking my father to go out and shop because he would just yell at all of us and hide the keys. At that time, my school work was always late, and I was getting OK grades. When my father left, my grades began to rise.

In the eighth grade, I had no reason to be bad, so I just remained a "good boy"—that is, until Maria Vallarta surprisingly asked me out. Saying yes was a bad choice on my part because I used most of my school time on her instead of on my schoolwork. During our lunch breaks, we would just kiss in the halls and hang out with her friends. In the beginning of the semester, I did poorly, but when she was out of the picture, I did better. I ended up with mostly B's and some C's, which seemed bad to me. After about eight months together, I ended up breaking up with her. In those eight months, she was my best friend, my girlfriend, and the cause of my bad grades, which was sad to say. After we broke up, I worked hard, asked for extra help, and my grades went up. That year, I ended up graduating from middle school with more than ten awards, including the citizenship award and the highest grade point average throughout middle school. After breaking up with Maria, I ended my final eighth grade semester with three A's and three B's, which made me happy.

Today, my school work is the same—I receive mostly B's, and I am taking AP classes. And, today, my father is still doing drugs. I talk to him and see him every once in a while. He is living with his parents, and my family and I are still waiting for him to get better. What I learned through my young life is that things happen, distractions come from all different directions, and you must learn to overcome situations in a way that will make you happy.

Elizabeth Erasmo

ADAPTING TO CHANGE

"They don't make sheep like that anymore." I like this quote because it's true. For example, if you ever had something you liked since you were small, and you wanted to keep it forever, you still end up having to throw it away because it starts ripping, getting old, and wearing out. I have had this happen to me a couple of times. Once I had this really nice, pretty, and comfortable shirt that I loved. It was black and said "Angel" in the middle. After a while it started wearing out and losing its color because it was black and because of all the washing. I went to many stores to try and find one exactly like it, but didn't because "they don't make shirts like that anymore." That's when you start to realize that you want to keep that item for as long as you can in the best condition as possible so it can last a very long time.

The quote also reminds me of friendship, because when you become good friends or best friends with somebody, you want to be best friends with them for as long as you can. After a while you get mad at each other for some ridiculous reason and then never want to talk to each other ever again. Then you realize that you will only have one one-of-a-kind friend like her.

In third or fourth grade, I was with my friend at the lunch desk, and we were mad at each other. I don't remember why we were mad at each other, but we were sitting right next to each other but with our backs turned. We stopped talking for about two days. After that, we started talking again because we realized we got mad at each other for something that was not important enough to throw our friendship away for. We are still good friends, and we still talk, but not as much as we used to. Your friends are your friends, and if anybody or anything makes you get mad at each other, just remember that it's not worth it to lose a friend because of a fight.

Accepting that "they don't make sheep like that anymore" is very important in a person's life because even if we don't like change, we have to deal with life and just move on. Things will always be changing. It's better to adapt to the change than to try to find a way to fight it. Changes are always around, always will be, and will never stop.

Mariam Hovsepyan

HOW RELATIONSHIPS CAN BE

A relationship that is very memorable to me is one that my brother Jora was in about a year ago. He met Armine at a friend's house, and when he saw her he knew he felt something for her. He told one of his friends that he had feelings for Armine. His friend responded, "If you like her, just play with her; don't take her seriously."

Later on that same day, Jora and Armine were in a room alone. My brother told her, "I like you." She got teary-eyed and said, "Please just don't play me."

My brother told me after, "Right when I saw those tears in her eyes, I thought to myself, *How can I play with her heart? She's just so precious.*"

Then he knew that he really did like her. But my brother and Armine fought so much. They were always arguing, but at the same time, they really loved each other. Their relationship reminded me of the movie *The Notebook*. One moment they were nice to each other, saying how much they loved the other, and the next moment they were fighting like enemies.

She was a very funny, sweet girl, and had her way of winning his heart by sweet-talking and teasing. Most of the time I would look at them and think to myself how much I wished I had a boyfriend. They argued almost every minute, but they had this crazy kind of love.

My family knew about their relationship and so did her family. I always thought that if both parents knew, then the relationship was serious and it must last; this had to be a "meant to be" kind of thing. That definitely did not happen. It was a good lesson for me: just because both families know about the relationship does not mean it is going to last forever.

They had an on-and-off relationship; every time they broke up, I knew that in an hour they were going to get back together. The way I knew was because they were always fighting, but I also knew that the love they had for each other kept them hanging on.

After a while, I became close with Armine, and that made her and Jora's relationship closer. She would come over, or I would go over to her place and we would all eat, laugh, talk, watch movies, or play games. We had a great time. My brother's closest friend also started going out with one of her best friends.

While the family was getting bigger, so were the problems. Armine started spending more time with them than me, so I just backed away. It would get to me at first; I would cry and worry. But then it became a regular thing, and like everything else in this life, we learn how to deal with every kind of pain. Most of the time, I would deal with it by trying to ignore it.

The problems between Jora and Armine got worse and worse as the days went by, and they would get jealous of one another. If he talked to a girl, she would get jealous; when she would talk to a guy, he would get jealous. They wanted each other all to themselves, without sharing. In my opinion, a jealous relationship is unhealthy and one that will have a hard time lasting or turning out to be a strong love.

It was like neither of them had their freedom.

I believe that in a relationship, most things should be fair and each person should give the other person space, but their relationship went on like this for months. Sometimes I would think, *Maybe they do not love each other, or maybe they are just attached to each other.* Sometimes we think we love someone, and that is why we cannot let them go, but in reality, it is just that we are attached to them, and that is why we believe we can't go on without them.

There are many reasons why this relationship is memorable to me. The main reason is because I was attached to them too, because there have been many times when we all went out together—either to the movies or to the mall or to each other's houses. I learned a lot from this relationship and tried my hardest to learn from their wrongs and rights.

Now I do think I can make a smarter choice in the future when my time comes to have a boyfriend. I think I can be wiser and look at the bright side and make a better choice. As the days went on, they became colder with each other. I guess they were tired of their arguments and their break-ups. I believe an on-and-off relationship has the least chance of lasting forever. By looking at their relationship, I noticed that one like this is full of problems; it is a very complicated thing.

After breaking up, my brother seemed to move on quickly. But Armine would call and cry to me and tell me how much she missed him. I felt very used by her when she would come to me. It was like she was coming to me only for him—not for me. It was very painful. I would try to keep it short with her. I learned that most guys are like Jora. They move on way too fast, and I find that very sad; girls will sit at home and shed tears for months and months until we realize that maybe it is not worth it after all.

A couple of months later, she seemed to move on as well. Sometimes I miss having her around, but at the same time, I am glad that all those problems are gone.

About four months later, they saw each other at Starbucks. They sat down and talked, he bought her a coffee, and they enjoyed it. I liked that they still remained friends after a year of being in a relationship. Most exes do not remain friends, which is very hard for both sides.

I have truly learned a lot from Jora and Armine's relationship, and that is why it is so memorable and important to me. I want to always try to make the right choice and always watch out for problems, like the kinds that they had. I hope reading this helps you realize how relationships can be and which one is wrong and which one is right, and which one to complain about and which one to be grateful for. I will always take their relationship as a life lesson.

Sid Gonzalez

HAPPY, JUST NOT FOR ME

I am really happy for my sister. She is seventeen and seems really happy with her boyfriend, who is eighteen. If you were to see them hanging out in the mall or anywhere else, it would not cross your mind that they are dating. They would seem like a couple of really good friends laughing and having a good time. My sister's boyfriend still acts like he's ten. He's not the best-looking guy, but he acts like it anyway. Before, I just thought he was dumb, but now I think of him as my younger brother. I still think he's kinda dumb, though.

When it comes to my real brother's girlfriend, I don't want to see, talk, or—even worse—hug her. My brother and she, who are both nineteen, have been dating for about as long as my sister and her boyfriend: a little over a year. They go to the same college about two hours away, so I only see him on weekends, if not less.

There was this time my brother made me mad because he was giving me another one of his lectures about my grades. He said, "Oh you're stupid, look at your grades," so I told him to leave with his girl if he was going to lecture me. He told me, "Fine, I will. Forget you! I'll go with her!" I didn't want to cry right in front of him so I waited until I got home.

She didn't necessarily have to do anything for me not to like her: it was natural. I mean, he's my brother and I'm his little sister. My mom and dad know that I don't like her; my mom doesn't like her either, and Dad doesn't care. On New Year's, Dad suggested I take a picture with her. She was hugging me, and I was just standing with my hands put together in front of me. My brother, sister, and dad were all suggesting that I hug her. I didn't say no, but my facial expression did, so they left me alone.

Later, I asked my brother, "Is it that obvious that I don't like her?" He said, "Yeah, you always send her to the back seat when we go to the movies, then you never say hi or bye when she comes or goes. Why do you hate her? She hasn't done anything to you." She doesn't know it, but she has. She has, in a way, taken my place.

You're with her for five days a week; you see her practically every day. On those two days that you come home you go out with her. When I asked you to play some Xbox you said sure, but you forgot or were too busy. When the family and I call to say hello, you say, "I gotta go now." I remember when she and I used to get along, that is until you started treating her even better than you do me.

I do not necessarily want them to part ways because they seem happy together.

I only wish you would treat me the same. I bet if she asked you to do something you wouldn't have "forgotten." When she calls, you have plenty of time, nothing but time. I have to remind you to say bye before you go back to school when I've known you longer, known you better. Why's it like that?

Zaira Martinez

ONCE HE'S GONE

I knew Manuel all my life—we grew up together. Manuel was sweet, kind, helpful, amusing, loving, and caring—a best friend. He was a sports guy, and he also enjoyed watching movies, hanging out with friends and family, and going to the park. He would do anything to put a smile on anybody's face.

It was the summer of 2006, and I was watching music videos, drinking a Rock Star, and eating Skittles. I had just been suspended from school for two days for fighting with another girl. I had tried to walk away, but the girl got up in my face. My mom was mad, but she understood I had to defend myself. All the same, though, I was still really upset.

Later that evening, Manuel came over, like every other day, wearing a pair of blue basketball shorts, a white T-shirt, and white Nikes. He noticed my sadness right away and asked me what the reason was. "I don't want to talk about it," I said. He understood, not bothering to ask a second time. Manuel got up and left. Ten minutes later, he came back, jumping right into the middle of the living room in a blue clown outfit: blue Converses, a blue nose, a blue wig, and his face painted entirely white. He also brought his puppy Pebbles. Pebbles was sad, he told me, and needed to be cheered up as well. Manuel began dancing and jumping, and then pretended to be trapped inside a box. Right away, Manuel put a smile on my face and made me forget about my school problems.

On June 27, 2006, at four thirty in the afternoon, we were walking together in the neighborhood of Hollywood Boulevard and Normandie Avenue. All of a sudden we heard gunshots. Three hit Manuel.

One bullet hit him in the back. The second hit him in the chest. The third hit him in the head. Manuel fell right into my arms. I remember asking for help. Five minutes later, the ambulance arrived, and I was able to ride with him. I called his mom and my mom, and they got to the hospital as soon as possible. About an hour later, they pronounced Manuel dead. At that moment, I felt like my world was coming to an end. I felt alone, with nobody to comfort me. It wasn't until that point that I realized the luxuries didn't matter—what mattered was love. Manuel would always tell me money wasn't everything, would always tell me I would never be happy with what I had because I always wanted more. He would always tell me that there were kids and families with worse problems than mine, and they were happy. I, on the other hand, had everything—but I still wanted more.

Since this incident, I've become a better person. Now, each day I wake up, I thank God for letting me have another day of life and for blessing me with the family I have. Whenever I do get sad or feel down, I start thinking about what Manuel would do if he were alive. He would tell me all the time: "You look better with a smile than with a frown."

Marina Babaian

ALL I HAVE ARE MEMORIES

I will never forget that morning seven years ago. What I thought was going to be a bright and sunny day turned out to be the gloomiest day of my life. My mother woke me up around eleven in the morning with the saddest look. I got dressed, trying to ignore the spikes poking inside my stomach and the goose bumps that made my body shiver. We went to my aunt's house, and as we drove I saw the cold tears run down my mother's cheeks. I asked her what was wrong, but she didn't answer. My mother just held my hand to comfort me for something that I didn't know was coming. When we got to my aunt's house she opened the door and stared down at me with pain and misery. She and my mother sat me down. That's the moment when everything changed. They dropped the bomb. They told me that at midnight my dad had gone to the hospital because something was wrong with his heart. The doctors tried and tried to help him, but it was his time to go to heaven. As I heard what they were saying I wanted to become deaf and not understand what they were telling me. I felt like the walls were coming down on me. I didn't know what to do. My best friend was gone. The man that I spent each and every single day with was gone. My father was gone. How was I supposed to live without him? Life just felt plain, my stomach felt empty, and my heart had a hole.

I felt like I couldn't go on. As I repeated over and over in my head what my mother had just told me, all the memories and all the special moments that I had experienced with my dad flashed through my mind. The memories told me that the good old days were gone and I would not see him anymore. All that were left were the memories; I couldn't live them or make more. I looked up at the sky, wondering where my dad could be and why they had to take him away from me. I looked outside the window. The world looked dead. Life was sad and lonely.

Days passed and the house was empty. There wasn't much talking at home. Then the day of his funeral came. I arrived at Forest Lawn, where he would be buried. A hundred people gathered like ants all dressed in black with faces of steel and sadness in their eyes. I had written a poem for my father. When it was time to recite it, I had to pass by my father's open casket to get to the podium. My heart was racing as I looked at his face for the last time. It would haunt me for the rest of my life. My heart flipped, stopped, and jumped, all at the same time. Tears filled my eyes, and it hit me—my father was gone. Each step I took was a step without my father by my side. I started the speech. My first words were "My dad." As I said those words, my lips dried and my throat hurt. I wanted to yell *STOP! What's happening? What had he done wrong?* But I read my poem. Then, I had to watch my dad go away. I sat there as the dirt was thrown over him. Each time felt like I was stabbed with a knife. The pain was horrible. I wanted to throw myself in there with him. I didn't see any point of living without him. My heart was numb, and I didn't want to watch anymore, so I turned away.

When I lost my father, I lost my childhood, too. I didn't think with the same childish mind I used to. The world I once thought would have a happy ending, was great and beautiful, changed. Now I understood that things aren't always what they seem. I knew that I wasn't going to have that perfect family. I wasn't going to have that father figure. It was just my mother and me. I wasn't going to be able to go to Griffith Park, the L.A. Zoo, and all my favorite shops. Many questions came to mind: Who would I dance with at the father-daughter dances? Who would I have those special father-daughter days with? Who would walk me down the aisle when I got married? Who would be there to remember all those special moments that not even a picture could catch? Those special father-daughter moments were out of the question. I would not be able to experience any of that anymore. That special world that my father and I had, those moments that were just between us and only we understood—they were gone; they are irreplaceable.

Christine Tatoyan

LOSING HIM

My grandpa was the only thing that mattered to me. When I was upset or sad, he would always pick me up and take me somewhere I would enjoy, like the park. He would never come inside our house to drink water, because we paid for it. He would also leave his car so my mom wouldn't have to find someone to take us to school, because we didn't have a car. Then, he would sneak and put gas in the car, bring it back, and park it like no one had touched it. He was not only my grandpa: he was a dad, a brother, and a friend. He was anything you could ask for. I loved him.

But that one day came, the day he had to leave me to go to heaven. I will never forget that day. My parents knew how much I loved my grandpa, so they decided to keep that one thing from me and not tell me when my own grandfather passed away.

I usually never sleep over anywhere. But one day, when I was at my cousin's, my parents called and said, "Christine, you have to spend the night." I wondered why. I screamed and shouted and I couldn't sleep. I didn't want to sleep. I had a feeling something was wrong, and I was crying so badly my aunt just brought me home.

It was the middle of the night, and there were a lot of people over at my house. I asked my mom why everyone was upset and crying. No one would answer me; it was like I wasn't there. Then I looked up at my television, saw my grandpa's picture, and shouted, "Mom, where is Grandpa?" They all looked at me, cried even more, and said, "He's gone."

The room started spinning. It felt like my heart had fallen out of my chest. My hands were weak, and I didn't know what to do. My knees felt like they had ten million pounds of rocks on them, like they were going to drop and I wouldn't be able to get back up. It was all a big blur. People talked to me, and I felt like they were talking to the walls. I didn't understand what anyone was saying: I didn't care about what anyone was saying. *This is it, he's gone,* I thought to myself. I burst into tears, and I kept telling myself, *This is a dream, nothing is real.* But, unfortunately, it was. The feeling of losing someone you love is the worst. It feels like your heart gets bottled up, and you can't let it out.

On the day of the funeral, no one took me. I begged and begged, but no one took me. I thought to myself, *I'm going to run there,* but I was afraid. I never had the guts to go, even though I thought my grandpa would somehow save me if anything happened since I was going to see him. I prayed and prayed so I could see him one last time, at least so I could say good-bye. Everyone went, and I stayed home.

Is he ever going to come back, or is this it?

Nobody should ever take anything for granted. People should love one another, because you'll never know who is going to leave life before you. When I was upset, I used to get his picture and ask, "Where are you? Can you hear me? Are you ever going to see me? Can I see you?" There was no answer, but I felt like he was by me all that time. Now, when we go to where he's buried, it's usually his birthday, Christmas, or Easter. I always make little cards, or paint an egg and take it to him. I know my grandpa sees and appreciates it, even though his lovely, soft hands can't touch it.

Claudia Velazquez

MOTHER'S DAY

My name is Claudia Velazquez, and I'm sixteen years old. I lived with my mom, my grandparents, and my uncle—until my mom passed away.

She worked at Kaiser Permanente, where she had many friends who liked her. One day, she left work early so we could go to the movies together. When she got home, she saw my bad grades in the mail.

She got mad and told me, "I don't want you to be getting bad grades. You told me that you were going to get good grades, and you lied to me. You aren't going nowhere with me." Then she told me to take a shower and said, "While you take a shower, I'm going to drop off some groceries for my friend from work. I'll be back." She never came back or called us.

I thought she was with one of her friends. My grandmother and I waited for her call the next day. We waited for her to come home, and she never did. Mother's Day was in two days.

My uncle, grandfather, and I were going to take my grandmother and my mom out for dinner. My uncle asked us if we wanted to go to the police station to ask about my mom. My grandmother and I went and spoke with an officer. We told him how old she was.

He said, "Well, she is old enough to know what she is doing. She is probably with her boyfriend."

We told him that her boyfriend was in jail. We filed a report and had to wait twenty-four hours. Forty-eight hours passed.

It was Mother's Day when they found my mom in an apartment, dead on the floor with a bag of groceries. We found out that my mom's co-worker killed her because she never wanted to go out with him. My mom didn't like him because she had a boyfriend already.

He took her life away, and he knew that she had a daughter. I was only thirteen years old, and he did not care about what he did to my mom and my family. My mom was my best friend and like a sister to me—she was everything in my life.

My uncle gave us the news about my mom. We were in the kitchen. I was sitting in a chair. I just dropped to the floor and started to cry. I ran to the bathroom and locked myself in there. I cried and felt like killing myself because my mom was gone, the one and only person who had been there for me when I needed her.

Then my grandmother and my uncle told me to come out of the bathroom, that it was going to be all right and not to worry. I said, "It's not my mom, it's someone else." I was upset with myself. I told my family that this was all my fault. My grandmother told me that things happen for a reason.

I did not understand what she was trying to tell me because I was focused on what had happened. I was really upset. Months passed and I missed my mom. She wasn't there for me. Then, little by little I was forgetting because the words that my grandmother told me were true.

Things do happen for a reason. My mom was tired of working for many years in different places because she wanted me to attend a good college. Another one of her dreams was to give me a *Quinceañera*.

One year later, on Father's Day, my grandfather passed away. He had been sick with diabetes for many years. By the end, he had tubes in his stomach because he had too much water in his body. After two weeks of being in the hospital, he told me that it was time for him to go with my mom. He said, "We are going to take care of you and your grandmother and uncles."

I cried, "No! Please, God, don't take him away from me."

He was like the dad I never had. My family made the decision to take him off the machines. I was really upset because God took away two people I loved with all my heart, but I felt guilty because my grandfather was really sick.

Now if you see me, I'm happy because I'm living with my grandmother, my mom's mother. I love her with all my heart. Now I'm in high school, and I'm proud of myself because I made it to tenth grade. Hopefully, I will make it to college and make my family proud. My uncle has a baby, and that makes me even happier because now I have more family at my house. He is like my adorable little brother, and I love him a lot. I love my family for everything they have done for me.

Ursula Pattimura

DECISIONS, DECISIONS

When a baby is born, parents usually forget their problems and are proud of their new family. A daddy gives his baby piggyback rides, and the mommy yells, "No, you'll drop her." We all wish to have a perfect family picture where we see everyone laughing, where parents give comfort when it is needed. I remember days when my family resembled that picture-perfect image. We would always go to the park, and they would push me on the swings. They held each other's hands non-stop and lay together on the grass. But now we're not quite that image anymore. My parents disagree with each other constantly and have fights that can be heard a block away. My family is breaking apart, piece by piece, and it's pulling me right in the middle.

My mom is very passionate about Christianity. She stomps around the house singing, "I'm free and the Devil's under my feet," and reading Bible scriptures over and over. My dad is an atheist and has an opinion about everything. Nowadays my parents live and sleep in separate rooms. They walk by each other as if they are strangers on the street. They never talk unless it's about divorce papers.

One night, I happened to catch my parents fighting. I watched and heard names thrown back and forth. Dark secrets were finally being revealed. Most of the slurs came from my mom while my dad was just sitting there acting clueless. I had so many mixed emotions. I wanted to get away from it. As I walked back to my room, I overheard my dad say, "One of these days, sooner rather than later, we will be officially over." I felt as if I were in a nightmare where I couldn't wake up. I usually don't believe what he says, but for a moment, I began to wonder how it would be living with one parent. Feeling as if I had abandoned half of my heart, I wondered whether one of them would date someone else.

After a month or two passed, my dad told me in the car that he had met with an attorney. I asked if it was another parking ticket or if he was suing someone. The stoplight turned red, and my dad looked at me and said, "No, baby girl, I just got back from speaking to my divorce attorney." I simply laughed and said, "Are you kidding me?" My dad said no and showed me the folders full of papers with signatures. I began to think that I wouldn't want to get married so I wouldn't have to go through the process of divorce. I noticed the papers had only his signatures. He told me he hadn't showed them to Mom yet, but he kept reminding her to hire her own divorce attorney soon. My dad told me he wanted me to have a better and healthier lifestyle and that the divorce was the only way to fix the problem.

I had a difficult decision to make. If I chose to live with my dad, I would have to move to Orange County. If I chose my mom, I would have to move back to Indonesia. Either way I would have to leave everything I once had and start making new friends in a new school and environment. I began to think about the future, how my life could improve, and who I trusted. Living with my dad would mean that I would have to sacrifice everything and start over, but if it's for the happiness of my dad I would give up anything.

Two weeks passed by, and one night my dad told my mom to sign the documents and that he wanted full custody of me. My mom went psycho. She said, "I'm Jesus' child, and she's my daughter too." I heard them calling me, so I walked into the room. They asked me whom I wanted to live with, and I was quiet. I was scared to tell my mom that I wanted to live with my dad. At that moment, I was uncomfortable because I hate being stuck in the middle, having to choose who I wanted to live with, as if I was saying who I loved more. With my dad on the left and my mom on the right, I just couldn't take it anymore. I stormed out of the room and told them to stop pressuring me.

My parents haven't divorced yet, but they are still in the process. I never thought I would be in this position. I have already made up my mind to let my dad take full custody of me, and I'm confident that I've made the right choice for myself. My dad and I help each other. He's the one whom I can run to for advice, and we get along well. I finally told my mom that I would love her no matter what, but if she wants me to be happy, she should let me go and live with my dad. It was so hard to look at her and tell her. I wondered whether she would still talk to me or whether she would still love me. I don't want to upset my mom. I don't want her to think that I'm a traitor. All I want is for my parents to have peace. For the sake of my dad, being away from my mom is the only solution for his happiness, and my mom's, too. I told them I love them both equally and neither one is greater than the other. Being in this type of position is tough because I stress out in school, then come home and have family problems. It's as if another ten pounds have been added onto my shoulders. Honestly, I wish that all the conflict would just disappear and that I would never be put in this type of position ever again.

Stephanie Gonzalez

NO HAPPY FAMILY HERE

Since I was a little girl, I have loved my mom more than my dad. I felt like my mom was there for me no matter what. People asked me why I hated my dad, but I was so small I didn't really know what hate meant.

As I got older, I realized that I disliked my dad because he was never there for me. I always felt that he loved my sister Cristina more than me. At the age of five, I found out that my dad and my mom's sister had an affair. The consequence of their affair was a baby boy. My dad and my aunt's relationship affected our family as we slowly began to move apart from one another. I felt as though I could never forgive him. One or two months later I found out not only that my dad had cheated on my mom with my aunt, but also that he had an affair with another lady. That affair had the same ending—a baby boy.

"How can he do that?" I asked myself. "He never took care of me. How could he keep on having more kids with women that weren't my mom?"

As the years passed, I eventually got over all that hatred. I thought he was done with the affairs. But when I was eleven, we went through the same story again, only this time, I found out as it was happening. It all started one day when he left his pager and I saw that someone had paged him. I told my mom.

My mom called that number. A woman picked up, and my mom asked her why she paged my dad. She said it was because that was her boyfriend's number. My mom was really upset and confronted my dad that same day. He denied everything.

Maybe a month passed before my sisters and I found out that the woman's beauty salon was just a block away. We decided to go to her salon and confront her. While I was walking, I thought of many things. Maybe she was lying and just

87

wanted to break my parents up. Maybe they had something going on, but it was years ago. As I got closer, my stomach hurt and my eyes got watery. Finally we stepped into the salon where she worked. She just looked at us and already knew who we were. I was so mad but didn't really say a word.

She looked like a drug addict—really skinny and ugly. My sister Cristina was talking to her about the problem, and my other sister Victoria was shocked at how the woman didn't seem to care about anything—like the way she said she was my dad's girlfriend, even though he was married. She didn't really care about how we felt.

"I'm not about to fight with little girls," she told us. As we were walking out, a client came in, and I told her that the hair stylist might take her husband away like she had done to my mom. The lady was confused and surprised.

We went back home. I felt like crying. There were no excuses my dad could give us. He came home a while later, and he was really mad. He was ready to hit us. We asked him how he knew about it if they weren't together. He said, "I saw her on the corner; it's a coincidence."

I noticed that my dad was cold-hearted and didn't care about my sisters and my mom. I didn't really care about him caring about me, because I knew that would never happen. Ever since that day, things haven't been the same between me and my dad. He is so far away from me, and I haven't talked to him in about a month. I actually thank my dad for not being a part of my life because I've seen how hard my mom works so we can get everything we need. I know I can count on my mom no matter what; she will always be there for me.

Karina Escalante

WITH A LOVING MOTHER, WHO NEEDS A FATHER?

How many times have you heard of a child without a father? Or of a woman who doesn't have enough money to feed her children? And how many times have you heard of children being abandoned by their weakened mother?

Why are their mothers so weak? Is it because their jobs don't pay enough money to feed their children? Or maybe it's because their cowardly husbands left them with the children and now they think they can't go on by themselves?

Well, guess what? They can take care of the children by themselves, and I have a perfect example.

My mom always knew that my dad was a "player," but she still married him. My mom and dad were married for about two years before they had my brother. Eight years later, my mom and dad found out they were pregnant again. During the pregnancy, my dad cheated on my mom with another woman, and she found out. I was two months old when my dad left the house, leaving her with an eight-year-old and a two-month-old. My dad never paid child support. My mom worked five days a week to pay for rent, babysitters, food, bills, and diapers and formula for her baby. She never gave up on me or my brother.

My brother and I have gone through a lot, but we've gotten through it. One day my brother got a hold of my father, and so my father called me. I was very surprised and excited. Jessi, my brother, went to Kansas just to see my dad, but once he got there my dad ignored him and my brother wasn't able to talk to him. When my brother came back, we never received a call or anything. Two weeks after, I tried calling him because it was his birthday, and it turns out his phone number had been changed. That made everything worse for me. I tried calling more and more but got nothing. I got depressed; tears led to thoughts, and thoughts led to actions, actions that weren't a good solution. I almost committed suicide because of the rejection I felt from my dad.

It was hard, but there was a good side to it. My brother and my mom showed me how much more they loved me, and that let me know that with a mother like mine and a very special older brother, I don't need a father figure. My mom has raised me and my brother in a very special way. She showed me and my brother respect and love, which to me are two of the most important things in the world. People always say that they feel sorry for me when they find out that I don't have a father. To tell you the truth, I'm OK with it. The good side of this situation is that my brother and I have never seen a big argument or domestic violence between parents, and we haven't had to go back and forth to get permission to do something.

Just so you know, if my dad was still with us, my brother and I would be low-lifes, druggies, alcoholics, or dead. My dad used to drink, and so we would've gotten into the habit. I thank my dad for leaving us because if it weren't for him, my mom, my brother, and I wouldn't have found God.

For all the women who are single mothers and think that they can't go on, here's the example that proves to them that they can. Just show your kids that you do love them.

Pamela Lopez–Ruiz

A STRONG MAN, NO MATTER WHAT

Sometimes, my heart sinks when I hear people say they don't have a father, especially knowing how much anger they have toward the "father" they have never met. It hurts because the person I look up to the most—my hero—is my dad.

My father is the man who makes my life complete. He is always there for me. I know this is weird, but I tell him everything. Most girls feel as if they can't trust their fathers because they are "overprotective." That's not my dad. He understands me, even though I'm a girl. He knows exactly what I am going through. He trusts me a great deal, and I would never do anything to destroy that.

Life without my father just wouldn't be the same. There was a time when I lived only with my dad because he and my mother had problems. She went to Guatemala, her birthplace, but since my sister and I are American we couldn't go with her. So, it was my dad who dressed me, fixed my hair, and fed me. His cooking wasn't that good, but he tried. My dad always tells me that during that time, when he would wake up to go to work, I would wake up with him and cry because I didn't want him to leave. The only way he could calm me down was by giving me a dollar. I don't quite remember what happened to the money; I guess I lost it. My parents resolved their differences, and we were once again a happy family.

The longest I have lived without my dad was two weeks. He left because he wanted to help his brothers and sisters in Guatemala. The first week was awful: I would cry myself to sleep wondering when he would come back. By the second week, I knew my dad would come back soon because he was always saying how our family is his world. Once my daddy came back, I felt as if all the broken pieces of my heart were quickly put together.

My dad is always giving the best advice. He leads me in the right direction. He is always saying how my education is very important. He says without an education we are helpless in the future. He always says we should appreciate how education is free in America. In Guatemala, he had to start working during his teen years because there was no money for education. I try to make him proud by getting good grades. This man has worked hard for my family. At first, we lived in a small apartment, but now, thanks to his hard work, we have a beautiful house. Not too big, not too small. It is just perfect. He says the house is for us when he dies. He wants to leave us something beautiful.

My father is my hero. He is an inspiration to me. He is my best friend. This man, Carlos Lopez, will be in my heart forever, and no one will take away all the wonderful memories I have with him or the new memories that will be created by his side.

Arlaine Ablaza

MOMMY'S GONE

It was one of the toughest and roughest times in my life. I would come home from school to find pillows and picture frames scattered all around the living room. My mom and dad fought, verbally and physically. I took my dad's side. I got upset at my mom all the time because I didn't like the way she was treating him. My mom had a habit of throwing things at my dad. Once, she tried throwing a vase at him, but I ran between them, so she ended up hitting me.

Another time, they got into a huge fight. She went to the kitchen, got a knife, and tried to kill herself in front of us. It all happened so fast—there was so much screaming and crying—my dad held her arm and took the knife away from her. When he did, all three of us began to cry.

Later that night, my dad dropped me off at my grandparents' house to sleep over. A few days later, I came home, and my dad was sitting on the couch, crying. He told me to sit next to him, and he gave me a really tight hug and said, "Mommy's gone." I didn't really understand what was happening, but I knew she wasn't coming back because all her things were gone.

Ever since she left, my dad would always tuck me in bed and kiss my forehead. I thought everything was OK, but I was completely wrong. One night, I had a hard time sleeping so I decided to go to the kitchen to get some milk. I was about to turn on the lights in the living room when I heard my dad crying. It broke my heart seeing that my own dad was hurt, and for that I ended up hating my own mother. My dad didn't deserve any of this.

I blocked her completely out of my life; I was glad I didn't have to see her. I spent my nights in tearful telephone conversations and my days in daydreams where we'd end up as one whole, happy family again. I talked endlessly about it. I wrote long emails to my closest friends. Sometimes, I saw her as the devil incarnate who broke my dad's heart in the worst possible way. At the very least, she deserved to be horsewhipped.

There were times when I analyzed every single detail of their divorce. I told myself that this was what was best for all of us, it was God's plan. But deep down, I still believed that she would come back, and I couldn't understand how this was all for the better when every day seemed more torturous that the last. I was hurt; I missed my mom.

It got harder as the days passed—not being able to be with her the way I wanted to be, seeing her so unaffected, and dealing with my broken and smashed heart. I tried to immerse myself in other activities. I filled my schedule with movie marathons, shopping sprees, and anything else I could think of. It worked for a while, but then there were times her memory would sneak up behind me on tiptoes, catching me in my most vulnerable moments.

I tried to show the world I was OK and that I was over what happened. I no longer went around with a big "I miss my mom sign" on my forehead, nor did I go around with puffy eyes and a tissue box. I tried to live my life as it was before the divorce. People thought I was doing great. They heard me laugh and they saw me smile; I seemed happy and I told myself I was. But in the solace of my room, where I tried to organize my thoughts and sort out my feelings, I had to admit to myself that I wasn't happy, that my heart still ached for something that could not be.

It's been years since the divorce, and things have gotten better. I realized it was for the best. There were valid reasons why they split up, and I became stronger and wiser. I lost and loved. I cried tears for the things that were and that could have been. I wrestled with love, hate, jealousy, and frustration. I took down and brought up my pride. I rebuilt my world without the person it used to revolve around. When I couldn't save myself from the depths of depression and self-pity, I turned to God for help. I'm still not exactly sure what I gained or how much I lost. Maybe someday it will be all clear to me.

Debbie Bautista

ALL FOR LOVE

"Are you happy?" asked my mom during one of her two-hour lectures.

She said happiness comes from everything, especially from having a family and money.

"Aren't you happy when you buy something you've always wanted?" she continued.

I said I was, but it wasn't anything out of the ordinary, and it didn't last. As a rebellious child, I never agreed with her much. I had different beliefs and opinions than she did, and that's why we were always so distant from each other. I knew that and wanted it that way.

"I hate you!" yell most kids at their parents.

I am one of those kids.

My mom, who's in her late forties, works full- and part-time jobs to support her four children. She drives us to school every morning and cooks breakfast, lunch, and dinner. She struggles to keep the glue from unsticking, from letting the pieces break apart, but still we are slowly cracking. My dad is out of the picture. He used to come back and forth like he was glued on and then ripped off the family portrait. I'm used to seeing the image that way, so it doesn't matter anymore. I used to blame him for not being with us, for not sending us money for support, and for my mom's poor life.

My definition of happiness is being with people you enjoy—their companionship, never-ending laughter, little inside jokes, deep secrets, and weird conversations that only you and that person can understand. Of course, I never included my mom in any of this. We always fought because of the trouble I caused. I wanted to be different from the rest of my siblings, especially my sister. She's the "perfection" my mom created and controlled. I didn't want to be just another clone, yet I never wanted to be a disgrace. I wanted to live my life my way, but she always thought she knew best. I fought with her more than the rest of my siblings combined. I hated the consequences of her long lectures: constant yelling and restrictions from going out with friends. But I had to live with it, hoping someday she would see me as me and not as my sister.

Sometimes, I feel horrible for the way I treat her. But I can't stop now; I can't give in. It's been a long war, but nothing will be resolved until she treats me fairly.

She didn't let me out much.

"Why can't I go with them?" I would yell.

"Because I don't know them!" she screamed back.

She was unreasonable when I'd try to fight back, but I'd always lose.

She's right, though. She doesn't know my friends, but she didn't take the time to know them. *So why bother,* I thought.

My mom thought everything with me was fine until she caught me in a lie. There was a secret I was hiding. All hell broke loose when she found out I really liked a boy in school.

"Mom, I like this boy," I said nervously.

"What's his name? How did you meet him? He's in your one of your classes? Umm, how does he look like? What do you like about him?"

She kept stuffing questions in a bag for me to pull out, like raffle tickets, but there was no way I would win a prize.

"Uh, James. Uh, he's everything, I guess."

It didn't make sense, but I didn't want to be specific. Plus, I didn't even know which question to answer first.

"Remember, no boyfriends, I told you, until after college," she snarled.

I already knew that; it was her first rule for my sister and me. But I had always wanted to experience having a boyfriend. It was my problem if I got hurt.

James and I were really close even though we constantly fought. "Puppy love," people called it. But how do you define love? Is it in the dictionary? Someone else's opinions? Selfish needs? Is it the struggles you go through that make everything solid and stronger? How do you know if it'll work or not? Was I too young to know? But should I have let all of these questions go unanswered because of my mom's ridiculous rules? I told her I was going to obey her, but I was lying and didn't let James go.

I hated the idea of keeping someone so special to me away from my mom. I couldn't always hang around with him when I wanted, but keeping our relationship secret seemed like the only way to keep us together. Then we began having arguments. My mom would notice when I was down, but I couldn't speak to her about my feelings.

Two months later, on my fifteenth birthday, James and I were walking home, holding hands, and my mom saw us from her parked car and just stared. It was a horrifying moment, and I knew I couldn't escape. I laughed to cover my fear, but inside I trembled, and I couldn't stop. I got in my mom's car and was quiet until we got home.

We sat on separate couches in the dark living room. Neither one of us bothered to turn on the lights. She started yelling at me in English with a mix of Tagalog, screaming about how disappointed she was in me. I sat quietly, trying not to snap at her because I knew it would only get worse. I let her keep yelling at me and asking questions, but I didn't have any answers.

"*Tanga ka.* (You idiot.) Didn't I tell you?"

"Yes." I looked down.

"Then why did you start going out there and get with him?"

"I don't know."

It's pointless, I thought. I couldn't tell her the truth: that I wanted a boyfriend, that I really liked him, and so I went with him. None of that was what she wanted to hear. I couldn't take her yelling anymore. It was making me mad, and I began to cry. She still kept yelling and repeating every sentence over and over again. It got worse when she threatened to kick me out of the house and send me back to the Philippines. She said she didn't want to deal with me anymore. I was sad and afraid that she would send me back to start living another way of life. But she couldn't read my mind, and she never understood me in the first place.

She was so angry with me that she left the house. I began to think that I couldn't live with her. I called my friend Ursula because she understood my problems. I knew she would be there if I needed a place to stay, but she didn't pick up. I was panicking. What if my mom came back before I had the chance to get out of here? What if she tried to stop me, or this fight got even worse? I couldn't think of anything else, and I knew I needed to get out. I didn't know the right thing to do, but it hurt me to know I had disappointed lots of people, including James. So I went to Ursula's house, hoping she'd be there when I arrived.

I was at her doorstep within an hour, and her mom opened the door. She certainly didn't expect me. Through the door, I saw Ursula walking down the stairs. I felt safe then. She knew the reason I had come, why I had my backpack, why my eyes were puffy and red, why I looked like an intruder on her doorstep. Her family let me stay, but James called and told me to go back home.

"I can't," I said.

"Debbie, your mom is threatening to call the police on me. You know how much trouble that would put me through? She keeps coming here, thinking that we're hiding you. Everyone is flipping out. Debbie, go home."

I could hear the disappointment and fear in his tone, but I just couldn't go home. I couldn't put myself through the things my mom kept putting me through. I wouldn't let it happen.

Later that night, my mom showed up on Ursula's doorstep and acted as if I had only come to Ursula's house to play with Barbie dolls and have a tea party. I was scared, and I couldn't even look at her. I didn't want to admit I was wrong, and neither could she.

"Sorry for all these problems," she said to Ursula's parents.

"Oh, no, no, it's OK. My daughters were like this, too," her dad said, focused on *American Idol.*

Ursula and I hid on the stairs, but her dad turned around and caught us. He told me to come down and talk, but I was full of fear. I still couldn't look at her; I felt guilty. Finally, she was leaving, but before she did, Ursula's dad told me to hug her. I didn't want to but they made me.

"I'm sorry," I whispered.

She told me to take care, then left. As she was walking out, she was probably thinking about how full of shame I should be, showing our problems to other families we hardly knew, how stupid I was for running away, how I had disgraced her.

The next night, she asked if she could pick me up. I let her. I was nervous to go home because I thought things would get worse. I thought she'd only send me to the Philippines. Once again, she had another lecture ready. I didn't want to get to a place where I hated my own mother for the things she did for me, either for good or for bad. But as a teen growing into an adult, I shouldn't have to be forbidden from certain life experiences.

We realized that our anger was pushing us both to the edge of a cliff and soon one of us would fall over. But we were both wrong. She came up to me, and I knew then that she wanted to stop this animosity, this selfishness, this war. I didn't want to appear weak, but I know I didn't want to go through these things again. It wasn't about winning anymore; it was about getting along with my mom. I've realized that my life could have been easier if I had not lied to my mom. After running away, my relationship with her changed. It's not easy to avoid an argument with a mother who has completely different views from you, but we manage. We're able to talk to each other, not only about school, but also about my feelings. She also accepted James as my boyfriend and has gotten to know my friends. It might have taken a while, but she started trusting me again, and I have been honest with her. We both got what we wanted from each other. She started treating me fairly and saw me as me, not as my sister. I changed my attitude and slowly opened up to her, including her in my life.

Jonathan Madrid

MY RELATIONSHIP

The day I looked to the other side of my fifth grade classroom and saw her, I thought she was the most beautiful girl I had ever seen. "She's the one for me," I said to myself.

In elementary school, for some reason, I had a lot of things in my little mind that I could not believe I thought about. Movies or things I saw on television made me realize I felt like an adult, or a teenager. I felt I had to have a relationship. It's funny, because after that I realized how beautiful girls were.

The days went by, and I had this big crush on a girl. I didn't know how to express it, because she was the girl all the guys liked in that class, too. This made it harder. But I was smart enough to tell her best friend, Rosa. If it hadn't been for Rosa, I would never have gone out with Jennifer. Valentine's Day was coming up, and I said to myself, "Get her something she would surely like." So, I bought her a teddy bear with some candies. Valentine's Day came, and I was so embarrassed to give her the bear that I didn't give it to her until a week later at lunch.

"Oh, you're so sweet!" she said. She then gave me a kiss.

Two days later, she stopped me, and asked if I wanted to go out with her.

I was like, "YES!"

We started dating, and it was paradise to me. It was like the movies.

If only I knew the problems that were going to come.

One day, a boy came up to me and asked, "Are you going out with my girl?"

"That's right," I said. "She's my girlfriend, not yours!"

Later on that day, he was crying. For some reason, she never told me she was going out with him, too! I felt bad for him, but I was in love so I wasn't letting anybody take her away from me.

When we got to graduation, she was angry at me because I was not letting her talk to any guys. We graduated, and she told me before she left to call her and to always keep in touch. We were going to be at different schools.

At the beginning of sixth grade, Jennifer told me she was moving somewhere else because of family problems. We still kept in touch, but I was afraid of where our relationship was going. I asked her if I was ever going to see her.

"I don't know," she replied. "I don't know if this is going to work out if I can't even see you."

She thought it would always work out, but I told her we should see other people because we were going to be in new schools, with new people, and it would be better for us. She agreed and told me I would be her "number one babe." The year went by, Jennifer was gone, and I was falling for other girls.

I had just started the seventh grade when Jennifer called. She told me we could finally see each other at her birthday party. I was so happy. We had not seen each other for a year, and she still considered me her boyfriend—so we made it official that we were still going out. We planned to go on a date to bring us back together, like we had been in the past. We went to see *Freddy vs. Jason*, and we were cuddling up. Then, we had the longest kiss ever. It felt like this relationship was never going to end. Then we had the weirdest conversation. She told me what kind of wedding we were going to have, how many babies we were going to have, and even their names!

I found out later from a friend that she kissed my enemy. I was so angry that I cheated on her. Then, we both explained to each other how we had cheated, and we decided to break up.

We haven't talked since the eighth grade.

Now, it is becoming harder to find a good relationship because it is difficult to know the true intentions of a person. It's becoming harder to see if someone is interested in you because of who you are or because of your looks and what you can give them. I have seen how a separation can take a perfect couple and turn them into a nightmare of a problem.

Wei Ming Tang

ONE HOUR TURNED INTO A LIFETIME EXPERIENCE

I stepped into a gang neighborhood one day.

It was a Saturday afternoon; my sister and I were walking to the local Los Angeles City College to apply for the classes that would enable us to gain additional extracurricular activity credits. Not aware of the daily violence that occurs in the neighborhood that we were about to walk into, we noticed a metropolitan neighborhood swiftly divide and transform into the "ghetto." Children in front of their apartments played handball with faces that did not show much emotion. Bald-headed teenagers sat on the front porches or leaned on cars, giving a death-defying look to passing motorists and pedestrians.

One gangbanger wore big denim jeans, a tank top, and bright white shoes, while his skin was covered from top to bottom in tattoos. My sister and I spoke in Cantonese with each other, so it looked as if we were foreigners not trying to cause any problems. However, with my eyes being sensitive to light, whenever the sun shines directly into my eyes, my eyebrows usually intertwine, giving me an expression as if I were looking for trouble. I had no choice but to arch my eyebrows up and look like I was amazed at how great-looking the neighborhood was, even though it was sprayed with graffiti and looked like a dump.

Loud reggaeton music flowed out into the streets and caused an echo. My sister was annoyed and secretly slipped on her earphones, so I was basically talking to a brick wall. I was clueless, because every ten seconds she would say, "Yeah. Yeah—Yeah." It seemed like she was agreeing with what I said, but she was actually singing to the lyrics of a song. As we got closer and closer to our destination, more and more pedestrians were around. There were young single mothers grocery shopping with their children in the afternoon. As we got closer and closer to another commercial area, we noticed we were nowhere close to Los Angeles City College. We were amazingly fortunate and found a subway that had tour guide brochures of where locations were. As it seemed like we were the only pedestrians lost in the flow of passing traffic, we quickly blended in and figured out the brochure. We had to walk back around the gang neighborhood we had just come from. We crossed quickly through changing street lights and gasped for air as honking horns beeped at us.

Gang members who saw us earlier recognized our faces and stood up from the porch as if they thought we were trying to cruise around looking for trouble. "No Cruising" signs are used by law enforcement to explain that no drug trading or cars looking for trouble are allowed. The gang member ran to the sidewalk and slowly passed to the street I was on. He spoke in Spanglish to my sister and me. "*Tu quiero marijuana?*" he said. We were totally clueless, and he raised his voice, breathing a heavy gas of marijuana and acrylic paint. Police cars approached, and the gang member ran through an alleyway. We were shaking in our pants and kept walking normally. The police car was occupied by an innocent-looking teenager and two police officers. The driver glared at us as if they were trying to find gullible teenagers to bash on.

Alexei Petrov

(VERY) PERSONAL

I am fifteen. I know how to breathe, to laugh, to exist. An existence composed of half-note wounds in legato and staccato. Memory without some constant ache— or *longing*—is blurry and washed-out like paint with too much water in it: weak, diluted, faded. Sometimes, at night—when I know no one else is awake—I feel like screaming. There is this pain in my stomach—cold, raw, relentless pain—churning the insides with such extreme intensity—*it's the longing, dear*—eating away my guts until I am sure there will be nothing left by morning—

Spinning, spinning—just a little faster—to the depths of degradation, clumsily.

The problem with humans, you see, is that we're more entranced with our fantasies than reality.

So, I dream because—seized by the neck, the flowers of poison *bloom*.

Sometimes, at night, when I feel like screaming and there comes the telltale muteness—the monotone of an indistinguishable existence—I wonder what it's like to stick my hand through someone's chest. A passing thought. A fantasy. The acid hiss of nails rending flesh, giving purpose, sketching me in vibrant colors. The white of bone, the crimson of blood.

I imagine the feeling of my hand going through human flesh, the layers of soft-ness yielding inwards as my flattened palm pushes further still, fingers extended long and straight in front of it. It is those fingers that would first encounter the *blood.* The resplendent claret that would coat everything, make them slick with life, and the loss of it. I imagine the blood gushing out to soak *everything*, splattering my cheeks, and filtering the world red. Pulling my shirt taut, and wet against my skin as I push my hand further still. This time, it encounters the bone, the hard-rib bone, that simply *shatters* beneath my power, small chips and shards bouncing off the adjacent ribs and each other. The anticipation almost deathly, I bury my hand—which is covered up to the elbow in blood so thick it is impossible to see anything beneath it—even deeper in.

My hand is impaled upon a living, breathing doll.

Grotesquely *resplendent*—

I gasp from sheer pleasure as I find my target, the wildly beating and fiercely alive target—the heart, that wonderful *thing* whose beat I would be able to feel coursing through the body I have impaled upon my own hand.

I pause to look at the face of the doll and see nothing but—

My fingertips twitch, catching on fragile vessels, and the intact pericardial membrane. The broken edges of white ribs claw upon my intruding hand. For a moment, I feel the ghost of a sigh across my stomach, like the skim of butterfly wings on top of honey petals—*almost like that feeling when you're in love?* But, it would only be *momentarily*, because the scream of frenzied, almost-painful anxiety—*Do it. Do it!*—overwhelms everything else. Finally, my fingers grasp that heart gently, delicately even, as though it is expensive china or a newborn baby's head, then would *crush* it, squeeze it, burst it open, lifeblood escaping that newly shattered ruin in massive spurts. The heady tang of copper *consuming* me, letting me reach heaven and change hell and then dragging me back to this—this—

I see the ceiling, and feel the heavy pulse of longing—
(What longing?)
nothingsomethinganything

It's a sin not to want things.
Desire is the key, a healthy longing, a wish for *life* with all your heart.
(Will you chide me now?)

The puppet strings draw taut again, jerking back the *almost*—almost because the bitter frown would not displace itself—ubiquitous smile I wear, like one wears rings and necklaces.
And tomorrow will be the same—
(Please explain your smiling face.)

I can only swallow down myself, and find life in dreams.

Morena Castellanos

FROM MARSHALL TO MY HOUSE

As I get out of Marshall High School, I see everyone go in different directions. Some take a bus, a car, or just walk. Since I walk all the time, I get to see things in many different ways: some things are just plain wrong while I find other things to be funny. By walking, I get to experience things in a much more detailed way.

As I walk home, either by myself or with my boyfriend Leo, I pass by a 7-Eleven and see many students waiting for a friend or family member to pick them up. As I keep walking I start watching how people split up into different areas. There is an elementary school, Ivanhoe, where I get along with many of the students. One student whom I see as a very trusted friend is Lupita. She makes me smile when I see her outside.

After I pass the school I see very organized, clean, appropriate houses, and I see it's a very quiet and respectful neighborhood. I go on past a Subway, a laundry place, and a hair salon. These are very useful places to have nearby, and it's perfect that you can find all three at once. So I go on, and there's a 76 Gasoline station near a church named Apostolic Faith. I find this very awkward, because I've never seen two places like that next door to each other.

From the church I keep going and notice the ampm. Right across from that is a Rick's Burgers, and across from that, a Chevron. I think it's funny that one block after the 76 there are two more gas stations. Then I walk over a bridge and notice the purple and pink lights of a gentlemen's club. I walk past the gentlemen's club and a couple of auto places. Across from them lies the LA River. The river stinks so much I think it's a mutation river: if you throw a clean fish in, it will come back out with three eyes. Once you get near the river, flies begin to attack. It's funny when I think about it. I see it as a joke.

From the auto place, I avoid the LA River and walk down to a place that smells good: a Hostess bakery. As I get near I like to slow down to smell the sweet chocolate in the air. After that, I have just one block to go to get to my house. As I pass a house that smells like onions and garlic, the sweet smell of chocolate goes away.

Now I just have to cross the street to get to my house, but that's when cars just go crazy, and they don't let me cross. Every time I walk across the street, there's a car that almost hits me. That bothers me because every time I have to pass, drivers lose their respect and forget they might hurt innocent young students on their way home from school. I find it interesting that people lose their patience so fast that it might get to the point of killing someone, even in areas far away from Marshall High School and my neighborhood; there are people who just don't care about students like me.

Meli Martinez

DIFFERENCES

Every Friday I travel from Marshall High School to my home in the city of Pico Rivera. On this journey, the environment changes from city to city. Like many kids, I have two homes. The house where I stay during the week is up on a big, steep hill. It is not too far away from my school. This neighborhood is a really private, quiet, and peaceful place to live. Our neighbors are older, and there aren't many kids my age. I like it, but at the same time it's really lonely, whereas my weekend house is lively with a lot of children of different ages. It is actually on a very busy and noisy street. Usually we take the freeway home from Marshall, but I like to go through the streets to see the changes in the environment and the people.

The neighborhood around Marshall is filled with nice houses and apartments. I see a lot of Caucasians in their twenties dressed like hippies and rockers. It bugs me to know that these Caucasians (who have money) are moving into homes where Latinos struggle with rent. Then we drive through Echo Park, where I mostly see Latinos. There are women with their children, walking or waiting at the bus stop. Echo Park looks very dirty. There is a lot of trash on the streets, and it kind of reminds me of Mexico because of the poverty—I see homeless people under bridges or by the freeway entrance.

At the park, I see many people running, trying to stay fit. Some are there to have fun, some are vendors, and there are others who are up to no good. This park isn't such a lovely park, but many people appreciate that it is there for them.

Then we go through downtown, where there are many tall buildings and businesses. There are also hotels, swap meets, and little shops. Then we go through a very horrible area: Skid Row. This place is home to many, many homeless people.

It is sad to see so many people living like this, whether they are men or women, young or old. They sleep on these streets in cardboard boxes or with whatever they can find to make their home, like blankets, broken furniture, or tents (if they're lucky). They beg for food and money and live off the streets. Some are on drugs, some are prostitutes, some are drunks, and some have other reasons for living in this condition. The lucky ones stay in shelters where they are fed and have a roof over their heads.

Skid Row is only a few blocks, but it feels miles long. This is a terrible environment that I see on my way home. It makes me feel very sad. I want to cry because it must be rough to deal with this lifestyle. Watching these surroundings through the window of our car, it gives me the creeps knowing that this could happen to anybody.

Next, we go through East Los Angeles. Like Echo Park, I mostly see Latinos. There are many Mexican restaurants along the streets. There aren't as many apartments, but there are a lot of decent-looking houses. I see a lot of kids playing around in their neighborhoods. We pass Roosevelt High School and see many students on the field practicing their sports like any other high school in any other city. I also see a lot of little shops like there are downtown, but here you see a lot of shops with things for *Quinceañeras*—dresses, tuxedo rentals, limousine rentals, bakeries, and many other party event shops. I love looking at all the dresses in the windows of these shops. It brings back memories from when I was preparing for my own *Quinceañera*. The people here seem to be very happy, and it makes me happy to see that! I feel like I'm in Tijuana because of all the shops and people who live here.

Once we hit the end of East Los Angeles I see a sign that says *Montebello*. Here are mostly well-maintained houses and very few apartments. The people seem to be very mellow and private. This city has many little parks here and there. As we go past Schurr High School, a couple of students skate in the parking lot or down a hill on that street. I feel very clean and safe when driving through this city.

Finally, once we cross over the bridge (it burned down last year) from Montebello, we end up in Pico Rivera. It is a very small city. It is surrounded by cities like Whittier, Downey, Santa Fe Springs, and Norwalk. There is only one high school because the city is so small. The houses here are really nice. On the north side of the city there are huge houses that used to be, or still are, ranches. When I go to the 7-Eleven, I see families riding their horses. I feel silly when I see this, as if I were on a farm. There are a lot of parks where many children are involved in sports and after-school activities. This city is very united. Most of the people here know each other because they were born or raised here. When I first moved in, I felt very left out, but over time I started talking to people. The people here are very friendly. You can see the people here are third- or fourth-generation Americans of Latino heritage.

On Fridays after school, I have a long ride home. But there are so many different people and sites I can look at to keep me from getting bored. Have you noticed the change in environments on your way home? If not, I suggest you pay attention to your surroundings and look at the details around you. I hope your way home is as interesting as mine!

Danny Reyes

GOING TO MEXICO

Every September since I was a baby, my family and I go to Jalisco, Mexico. We drive to El Paso and stay in a hotel to sleep for only three hours. As the sun comes up, we are crossing the border into Mexico. I grow more excited as we get closer because I'm going to see my grandma and grandpa. Mostly I am excited to see my horses, cow, and fighting rooster.

We have parties in the town with music and bull riding and horse dancing. All my horses do different things. There is one horse named Pinto; he is black with blue eyes and white covering his face like a mask. My grandpa is a horse trainer and taught Pinto how to act dead, dance, and turn one leg.

Every September 19, the town goes to a special place by the lake to have barbecues and to play games. The guys go on horses to find girlfriends. I was there five years ago with my brother, cousins, and uncle when the bees went crazy. They were really big African bees and killed people. We ran back to the truck and didn't get hurt. The next day people were selling videos of what happened at the party, and I thought it was messed up because people died.

This is what happens when I go to Mexico.

Sandra De La Cruz

MY TRAGEDY IN MEXICO

This is how my life changed. My family and I were really close until a tragedy happened three years ago. My parents, my two little brothers, and my little sister went on a trip to Mexico. My older sister and I stayed home.

It happened as soon as they got there, while my brothers and my uncle were horseback riding. My brothers were off to a good start, but all of a sudden my uncle's horse got scared and jumped back. A kid ran to where my parents were staying and told my dad. He ran out the door looking for my two little brothers. When he found them, one of my brothers was badly injured. My parents took them on the hour-long drive to the hospital, but on the way my brother Bryan passed away. There was nothing else to do but take him to the hospital and wait until they could bury him.

My sister and I found out while we were at my cousin's house. A lady from Mexico called my cousin, Irene, and told her. Irene broke down in tears. My sister got on the phone and asked what happened, and the lady told her. Then I got the phone and she told me. My parents didn't want to tell us because they were worried about how we would react; they wanted to tell us when we got to Mexico. We got on the next flight.

Now when we talk about Bryan my mom and dad break down in tears. I don't like seeing them like that because it hurts them and their health. It took us a long time not to cry over Bryan's death as much. It has been three years now, but I still think about what Bryan would have been doing right now. I imagine him playing with my dad, but then I see my dad sitting on the sofa with my mom. I just wish I could have him back so I wouldn't have to suffer what I'm going through. I would never wish this upon anybody. If I had the chance to get my baby brother back I would take it, but I know that's not going to happen. So instead, I pray every single night for him and for my family so that we can all be safe and keep on going with our lives.

Jannet Gurrola

MY PARENTS HAD IT EASY

Twenty years ago, my father came from Durango, Mexico in hopes of a better future for himself and his future family. Before my father came to the United States, he met my mother, who was working as a housekeeper. She also took care of her brothers and sisters. It was very benevolent of her, but she still did not enjoy doing it. When my father met my mother, he repeatedly thought of her and eventually fell in love with her. He asked her for her hand in marriage, and my mother instantly replied, "Yes!" Then my father sent money to my mother so she could buy her wedding dress. When they got married, they threw a big party. Years later, my father asked my mother if she wanted to go to the United States so they could have a better life for them and us, their future children.

Years after they finally came to the US, they had my brother, and a year after that they had me. I know my dad is happy with us. When we were little, he used to buy us whatever we wanted. My parents also threw us big parties, and my dad used to take us out to eat. He knows that we are big, but he still loves us. He tells us that he wants a better life for us. My parents have started telling us that when they die, they're going to leave us whatever they have.

I'm happy that I have good parents who tell me to work hard at school so that I don't have a nasty job like cleaning restrooms. I want to try my best in school so that my parents will be proud of me.

Elizabeth Chavez

A JOURNEY FOR HIS FAMILY

I want to tell you a story about my father and how he came to the United States. My dad had to leave the small city of Zacatecas, Mexico, his loved ones, and all the things he had. Leaving everything in his homeland and going to start over in the United States was going to be hard for him.

My father came to the United States for a better job. The economic situation was very bad in Mexico, and my dad's family was poor. My father was paid ten dollars a week, and he would eat two meals a day of beans, rice, and tortillas. Food in Mexico back then was expensive. Sometimes they would also eat meat, but only once a month because they couldn't afford to buy it every day.

My father got his first new outfit when he took his first communion at the age of eleven. Usually, Grandma would buy the oldest brother clothes, and when his clothes got too small he would give them to the next brother. Since my father wasn't the oldest, he wouldn't get new clothes. Grandma worked really hard to buy my father his first outfit, as she did for the rest of her kids.

When my father was two years old, he lost his father. It was a really rainy day, and there was thunder and lightning. My father's father was working in the fields, and suddenly lightning hit him and killed him. This was very tragic for the family. My father has eleven brothers and sisters, and my grandpa had just passed away and left Grandma with all the kids. Grandma was in shock, and for the next two months she tried little by little to get over the death of her husband.

Life went on for them, as it goes on for everyone else. Grandma started to work really hard every day, and never gave up. She would wake up at four in the morning to cook tamales and hot chocolate for two hours. She would then leave home at seven and go off to sell the tamales to earn money to feed her children. She was a strong person, always finding a way to make sure her kids had bread on the table.

My father had to stop going to school when he was a teenager because he had to help his mother and his younger brothers and sisters. Of his other brothers and sisters, three had already been married. Since they were no longer living there, he was considered the oldest, and so he had to help his mother. My dad started to work at the age of twelve. He fed roosters, pigs, horses, chickens, and all kinds of other animals. The money he earned helped his mother meet the needs of their home. When my father was seventeen, he lost his job. The men who had given him the job made plans to move to another state. It was hard for my father to get a job because of his age. The economic situation became more difficult for my dad's family because only Grandma was working.

When my dad turned nineteen, he decided to go to the United States. His decision depended on what he wanted to do with his future and what was best for his family. He wanted a good job, but he had his doubts. Leaving his family and going to another place was not easy for him. Seeing his family in need made him decide. His brother was ten years old, and he needed clothes and money for his education. My father didn't want his little brother to stop going to school like he had—he wanted the best for his little brother. He always thought about his family.

My father came here to the United States to start a new life and to work. It was hard for him to get used to this new country. He had to get used to the time difference, which was two hours, and being away from family. My father didn't know anybody, so he felt alone and sad. But he never gave up. He had a job already because his uncle had found him work as a busboy at The Cheesecake Factory. He usually had to clean up and wash the dirty dishes. Time passed, and my father was able to help his family by sending them money. He was a big help to them, and they were always thankful to my father. My father was happy he was able to accomplish that goal. Later on, my father got married and had a family. My father never stopped helping his family in Mexico and always kept in touch with his brothers there.

Christian Giron

INSPIRATION

I was born second of three brothers. There are many differences between my brothers. My little brother is sick, physically and mentally, while my older brother is crazy and in better-than-average physical shape. This makes my older brother unbelievably cocky and a troublemaking jerk, but he believes in family values, so I can call him a stupid jerk and get away with it. As for me, I'm average. I don't have any health problems to slow me down, or super powers to do the opposite. My big brother makes my mother angry, and my little brother gives her sorrow and makes her worry.

What do I possibly give her? Security.

My mom told me a lot of things that could have gotten her in trouble, which makes me mad. She once told me that there was a lady who wanted to buy me when I was still inside her fat belly. My mother agreed. She was very poor and was new to the United States. During the trip from Guatemala, my mom was very ill and took medicine that may have hurt me or caused a deformity. (If you know me, then you can decide whether it did.) My mom received housing and was fed healthy food for me, the baby, which made up for the medicine my mom took when she was pregnant. But back to that crazy lady. I have not been told why she wanted a baby. I don't want to know, but that lady and her food may have saved me.

I'm with my natural mommy because when I was born, she saw me and couldn't let go. She wanted to make me happy. So she ran away to LA. There, she told me, she received grueling comments, and she worked multiple jobs that weren't very fun. One of the ladies my mom worked for was an aunt of mine on my dad's side, who was very mean. Then, when I was a baby, we lived and slept on the streets.

But I didn't cry a lot, and my mom said she was very happy. She made friends, and we would sleep over at their houses. She said the only thing she lived for was her new baby boy. When my mother finally found a home, where I could sleep under a blanket in a cradle, that's when I started to be a baby. That's when I started to cry.

Later, when I was four or five, I got lots of attention, that's for sure. My mom lived in a house full of people, and it was good. It took years to get here: I was her inspiration, I was her happiness.

Sandra Castillo

LESSONS FROM MY PARENTS

My dad's name is Evodio. My mom's name is Sandra, and her second name is Mabel. My parents got married at a young age, when my dad was nineteen and my mom was sixteen. Now, my mom's thirty-two and my dad is thirty-six. Even though my parents are young, I have learned a lot from them.

They have taught me how to appreciate what I have, how to fight for what I don't have, how to be a healthier person, and how not to be selfish. They have taught me the most important thing in life is getting an education because it's the only thing that is going to help me in the future. They are always telling me to do well in school and to get good grades, so I can get my high school diploma, go to college, and get my career. They tell me not to waste time with a guy because then I'll end up depending on him.

Even though my parents are young, they have taught me a lot of things that people who are much older don't know. My mom is always telling me that when an adult tells an adolescent not to do something, the child is still going to do it again. "It's like you are basically saying, 'Yes, go ahead and do it.'"

So, every time that I do something wrong, my parents call me over and sit me on a chair and start talking about the issue or problem. They don't yell at me or hit me; they treat me like an adult. All they do is talk to me, and then I know that what I did wasn't good and that I shouldn't do it again. Some parents yell at their son or daughter, and their child ends up running away from home. That's why my mom says it's better to talk than to hit or yell.

All these things my parents tell me are things I will never forget.

Violeta Papazyan

WE TALK ABOUT STUFF OR WE TALK ABOUT EVERYTHING

It takes a long time for some girls to realize that a mother is a girl's best friend. I would never have imagined I would choose to be close to my mother, share my secrets, or even just talk about stuff.

My life was all about friends, fashion, and going out. It was easier to open up to my friends since they're my age and think more like me. You wouldn't get the same advice about a problem from a friend as you would from your mom. For example, let's say you ask your friend, "Oh my God, my boyfriend has cheated on me. Should I get back with him?" Your friend is going to say, "Yeah, you love him. Just give him a chance." But your mom would be smarter and probably help you get over him. At that moment, your friend's advice would sound much better to you because that's the advice you wanted to hear, but when you look back on it, your mom's solution was the right one.

Looking at my friends' relationships with their moms made me envious. I have one friend whose mom knows everything about her. One day, when I went home with her, she just started talking about her problems and completely opened up to her mom. It seemed weird to me because I never had that experience with my mom. Instead of talking about her problems with her friends like I do, she talked to her mom. She made the right choice because her mom helped her out a lot and gave her good advice.

As I grew older, I realized that life is not all about friends, fashion, and going out. You need a person to trust who will help you get through life and give you the right advice. That is when I realized I needed my mom as my best friend and that our relationship was not the way I wanted it to be. I think this had more to do with me than it had to do with my mom. My mom is a very understanding and caring person—I just never gave her the chance to listen to my problems.

One day, my mom and I went for coffee at my friend's house. We sat and just talked about stuff. For once, I felt close with my mom. I realized she had been a teenager, too, and faced most of the same problems I have. One of the things we talked about was friendship: how you can't always trust everyone that comes into your life and how you have to make the right choices when choosing friends. My mom and I had very similar thoughts and opinions about this. We agreed on everything and understood each other's views. After that day, I started to talk to my mom more and explain my problems to her.

My relationship with my mom now is much better than it was before. I spend more time with her and talk to her about stuff I realized she has more experience with. It's not as hard to talk to her as it was before. I don't think my mom changed so much; I think I did.

Susana Lobo

RELIGION AND BOOKS

Not once did I think what I read would make my parents nervous, much less that my reading would become a religious matter. I thought if I read they'd be happy. But, over the last few years, my parents have questioned me about what I read and the religion I am part of.

It all started two or three years ago, when my parents took me to see a movie. I can't remember the title, but it was a horror movie. That's when my interest in writing began. At first, my main genre was horror, scary things. I was good at telling these stories to several of my friends, mostly at night. I thought about the nightmares that entertained me. But, whenever I wrote, those stories would only come out in short, cramped, choppy paragraphs. I decided I needed to read some horror stories and find out what made them better than mine.

These books had pictures of vicious werewolves and titles such as *The Trails of Death* or *Vampire's Assistant*. Some of my favorite books would have to be the *Cirque Du Freak* series, which had vampires—that made them good horror books. My parents disagreed. They told me it wasn't healthy.

At first I was upset, but I ignored their demands. But then, as they became stricter about what I could and couldn't read, I began wondering why. Why would they hold me back from these books? Finally, I asked my dad.

"Because those books of yours are demonic. They corrupt your mind," my father replied.

I frowned when he told me this. Books aren't demonic. They are the reason I write, the reason I hope. They help me in school. But I decided to look at things their way. Sure, they were about demons and vampires, but that's what I'm drawn to. So when they saw me getting books like that from the school library, they got upset. I tried to explain to them that they inspired me, made me want to write.

"Are you ashamed of being Christian?" they responded.

That question caught me off guard. Why did it turn to this all of a sudden? I didn't understand them, but I stayed silent. They took it as a way of my saying yes, but I just didn't know how to respond. I learned then that to answer is better than to not speak out at all.

It eventually got so bad I had to read romance for a long period of time. But since I didn't have the money, nor did I wish to spend my own money on them, I ended up borrowing from my friends. I never liked romance that much, and when I began to read my friends' books, they scared me. There were too many steamy love scenes. It made me wonder to myself: *Why am I reading this?* If my parents knew they'd blow their tops. But I didn't show it to them. If they read this one, they might have gotten me those books they thought were educational. I kept the story to myself and only showed them the book's cover.

I had a routine. I could only read a horror book after I read at least two romance novels. There are no words to say how much I suffered because of this. But eventually I got used to them, and soon I was able to read a whole book in less than three days! This came in handy for when I wanted a book really badly. I'd read a romance novel in about three days, and then ask my parents to buy me the book I wanted. It worked well.

When I thought things were back to normal, I began writing short stories. But I kept them to myself for fear that someone would give me negative feedback.

My parents believe my books are a way to hide my shame, to hide my religious background. They believe I am simply avoiding my family's religion, that I'm ashamed to be Christian. I never was. But then a thought crossed my mind. *Which is more important: my books or my religion?* I decided I couldn't let go of my books. So I continued reading them, and my parents continued to tell me they were demonic. I sometimes wondered what would happen if they knew I wanted to become a horror story writer, or whether they were ashamed of me.

Whenever we went to a bookstore, I'd have to ask, "May I read this?" and wait for their verdict. Most of the time it was no. I couldn't get a book eighty percent of the time. I nearly gave up on them.

I began to think a lot about who I was to my friends and my parents. To my friends, I was a colorful gothic chick who enjoyed a good horror novel. To my parents, I was either a Christian or a girl possessed by an evil demon. It made me wonder whether my parents knew me at all anymore.

When high school started, I made new friends who shared the same interests as me. I borrowed books from them and read them in school. I didn't take them home.

My parents knew but slowly backed off. I was free to read without fear that my books would bring up religion. I still have to borrow books, and there is still that tension between my parents and me, but I hope they get over it before I tell them what I want to be when I grow up. To me, the thought of losing my books is the scariest story I could think up.

Margareth Lobo

A KNOWLEDGEABLE SEPARATION

Being a high-achieving child made it easy for me to excel in school, but at the same time, it was hard for me to interact with my classmates and parents. When I was in kindergarten, my teachers gave up on me because I "didn't have potential or enthusiasm to learn." My mother then put her jet-packs on and took over what my teachers wouldn't do. My parents taught me that in our Salvadoran culture, we always do our homework first and then are free to do what we please after we are done. My mother taught me to read with the book she had learned to read from when she was my age. This not only helped me catch up to the other kids, but boosted me ahead of everyone.

My parents were happy to hear that I was getting good grades and that I had even skipped second grade because of all my hard work. Even though I was achieving my parents' dream for me, they started feeling like shadows—close but untouchable. I would ask them for help on homework problems, and sometimes there was no response because they were busy with errands and bills. At other times, they just didn't understand the math problem or the "big" words in the text. I felt distant from them. I already felt this way with my classmates because of my focus on learning, and neither of my parents graduated from high school, so it wasn't like I was surrounded by scholars who could offer their support.

By the time I was in fifth grade, my parents, no longer together, felt useless, as if they couldn't help me anymore.

At school people felt uncomfortable around me. For reasons I didn't understand, I started getting abused at school physically and mentally. All the boys would pick on me and make fun of me. Some girls just didn't like me and wondered why

I hated them; they were awful, just plain mean. They would laugh at me, push me, and say random things about me. I would cry when I got home and then sleep all day because the last thing I wanted was contact with the cruel outside world. My parents knew about it, but they didn't grasp why this was happening. They believed it was children's play. My parents also believed that this knowledge I had gained would open new opportunities for me. It did, but I got hurt for it.

After my parents' separation, I went to junior high. Things changed quickly and affected me at school. My mother, remarried, had gotten pregnant with her third child. I was getting more social around people. But the second I left school, I dropped that character; I would become that depressed person, especially with my parents. They would sometimes complain that I should talk to people more. At times, I would be really happy at school, and after I got out, I would think about my day. But the second I got in my mom's Tahoe, I would become an invisible person who only looked out the window until she got home. My parents knew little about what really happened during my junior high years. When I hopped into the car and looked at my mother's face while she asked how my day was, I would give the briefest review on what happened, then stay quiet. I sometimes didn't even want to answer but had to make them happy. I felt so bad just looking at them force themselves to ask the painful question—"How was your day today?" I believed that my parents not only felt useless, but tired of having to deal with their children.

My mom would always tell me about her job taking care of Violet, the daughter of Jill (a photographer) and Robert (a producer), who gave her tickets to movie premieres and took her to her photo shoots. I was then in high school, and my mother had told me to come to Violet's second birthday party with her. I already knew Jill and Robert from when my mom took me to help her out, and they heard exceptional things about me from my mother. I didn't know that a small talk between Robert and me would change the way I looked at school.

Robert came up to me and asked how school was going. I said that some people at school wanted me to fail because I was too smart for them to handle. He said that junior high was one of his favorite times and that he enjoyed it; high school was even more exciting, and I should join sports or extra activities that might show my talents. My mother was there, listening in on what we were saying. He was giving me tips on what to do and what to expect when I got into a college. Robert did what my mother couldn't do and helped me realize how important it is to be very good at school.

I wanted to achieve more than my parents. I wanted to pursue a life that didn't even come close to what I have now. Other people in front of me had what I wanted and they didn't realize how people wanted to be them. I wanted to be them. My mother and father worked their butts off at their jobs, but Jill and Robert were people who went to school, studied, and became what they wanted to be. I kept looking at my mom throughout the conversation and saw her mixed emotions: happiness, confusion, and sadness.

After the party, I looked back on what Robert had told me. The ride home was very awkward. My mother broke the silence when she asked what I wanted to be. I still didn't know, so that was what I said. Then she started reviewing what Robert said. It hurt me when she was talking about it because of how she was handling the information. She said she didn't want me to go to her job anymore because she didn't want me to follow in her footsteps. I started arguing that I would never be a babysitter because I knew I could do way better than that. My mother was happy that I would strive for a successful career, but she was still worried. Thoughts started flowing through my head about what I wanted to be. I started feeling positive towards myself and my parents. I know that my parents will never stop helping me, but I couldn't help thinking that even if I do become successful it will be harder for them to connect with me. I knew that this scholastic journey wouldn't be easy, but I would try to share the experience with my parents.

I won't have a strong connection like other kids and teenagers have with their parents. My parents won't say "Oh, I was like that in my college days…" or "My prom was worse than that…" I will be someone with too little time to reflect on the past, only thinking about what's ahead. But I will be someone who represents my Salvadoran culture, and my dissimilarity in education with my parents will inspire other kids whom I will encounter. I'll tell them that just because their parents were at a disadvantage doesn't mean they will fail as well.

I felt as if my parents and my classmates were holding me back because they were afraid to see me in all my glory. By meeting Robert, I learned that instead of having no help, I would have support. Instead of fussing over not having parents I might have wanted, not having the same connection or memories other students might have, I found I would have other people to share the experiences with.

Rodrigo Guerra

A LIFE WITHOUT A MOM

My life without my mom has been very difficult. I don't like it when I wake up in the morning and know that she's not there to say "Good morning." My life was perfect before my mom left this world. I was a happy kid. I used to hug her, kiss her, and talk to her about my problems, but now I can't do any of those things. A mother's love is one of a kind. A woman can replace a mother, but that woman can never replace a mother's love. A mom's love is too strong to replace. When I see kids with their moms, it makes me sad because I don't have mine.

I was eight years old when she died. I would love to go back in time and tell her that I love her and that I never want to lose her, but I didn't have the time to say it. I was still a kid.

It makes me mad when kids say bad things to their own moms. Some friends have been telling me that they hate their moms and regret what they say to them. And I don't like when people talk bad about my mom. It makes me mad because they don't know where she is. When I tell those people that my mom is dead they say, "I'm sorry," or "I didn't mean to say that," but it's OK because they didn't know anything. I tell them to not to talk bad about someone's mom without knowing her.

It has been almost eight years since my mom died. I always stare at her picture to make me happy. But it makes me more sad, and I start crying. I used to be sad most of the time, but then I said to myself that I'm strong. The pain is still there today, but I can't do anything about it. My friend recently lost his mom. I told him that he has to be strong and not to let anyone bring him down. I would tell that to every kid who has lost their mom.

Aydhee Carrera

MI MADRE LINDA, MI MADRE ADORADA

To me, my mom is the most important, beautiful, loving, and caring person in the whole world. She is always there when you need her. She's always there to support you, always there to hold you when you can't stop crying. She's the one who will watch over you for all eternity.

My mom left Durango, Mexico, in 1980. At nineteen years old, she was headed to Los Angeles. She was a beautiful, young, five foot three inch young lady. She said that arriving in this new country was very exciting yet scary at the same time. But she got used to it. As soon as she arrived, she started working. She worked in a clothing company called Shades of California, Inc. She was in charge of arranging the clothes by sizes. In 1985 my mom met my dad. They both came from the same country, and they had much in common. Four years after they met, they got married. My parents' first son was born in 1989. Two years later, I came along.

I was born on October 19, 1991, at 6:30 a.m. on a chilly Saturday morning. I was my mom's first daughter. She called me *mi bella princesita* (my beautiful princess). I was my mom's little princess, and she promised to raise me in such a way that I would grow up to be a generous, helpful, successful woman.

When I started kindergarten at Micheltorena Street Elementary School, my mom came with me. I told her never to leave me. I wanted to go back home and help her with her house chores and play. She told me, *"Te tienes que quedar. Aquí vas a jugar, aprender, y conocer a muchas amigas."* (You have to stay. Here you are going to play, learn, and meet many friends.) I felt so sad that I wanted to cry. I felt as if I was being forced to stay there against my will. *It's not fair,* I thought to myself. *Why do I have to stay here while other kids are playing at home?* I was furious and sad, but there was nothing I could do. I finally gave in, but I still told her to stay with me until I told her it was OK to leave.

As I grew up, I began changing and thinking differently. When I was ten years old, my mom and I didn't have the same relationship that we did when I was younger. She would say, "*Limpia esto, recoje el otro.*" (Clean this up; pick that up.) I would refuse, and we would argue. "I hate you!" I would say. "I wish you would just disappear!" But I didn't really mean it. When I got over my grudge, I would go to my mom and apologize. She would always receive me with arms wide open. When I think about it, it's sort of strange how my friends say that they can't talk to their moms the way I do. It makes me be grateful that I have my mom to talk to about everything.

When I hit puberty, I began changing both physically and mentally. The first time I heard about that awful subject was fifth grade. We saw a horrible movie about girls complaining all the time about every little thing on their bodies. The movie was so graphic I was scared out of my mind. I had so many questions. Why do we hit puberty? What's so important about it? Why do girls suffer more than boys? It was a river of questions no one could answer. I needed answers and I needed them now, so I decided to talk to my mom. My mom and I had a very long conversation about everything. She explained how and why my body would change and answered all those questions. I felt so much better.

My mom is the most important person in the world. She has always been there to guide me through right and wrong. I've learned a lot from her. I've learned to never give up, to try my best every day, and to follow my dreams and succeed. She taught me to stand by myself without her being there. She taught me respect and about being a woman. She's the one who has always been with me and will continue to be forever.

Gayane Serobyan

A BLESSING

The definition of a best friend is someone you can turn to for anything: two a.m. phone calls that last until sunrise, sleepovers, and secret sharing. Throughout the good and bad times they will always stick with you, love you, and never judge you. I know this because I have so many friends but only one best friend: my mom.

My mom and I have a bond that cannot be broken. If someone had asked me a few years ago if I considered my mother my best friend, I would have laughed hysterically, but when I think about it, she has been my best friend my whole life.

Even though the beginning of my life was hard as a premature baby, my mom's love helped me through it. My childhood was not exactly a fairy tale. It was hectic and full of arguments and yelling, but every tear I dropped was wiped away by my mother. Life went on dramatically for the next thirteen years. It was very hard at times, but it also had its moments of happiness. As if life was too plain and simple and needed a turning point to liven it up, the divorce happened. Again my mother was there to hold my hand and be strong even though I was supposed to wipe her dreaded tears and bring joy to her face.

Life without a father figure was one of the hardest challenges in my young life. It was as though a new hole had popped in my heart. My mom always tried to fill that hole emotionally, physically, and materially. I will always love the warmth of her touch and the way she held me tight when I had a bad day. She tried to push my pain away and dried the endless tears that spilled from my heartache.

Life didn't go back to being the same for a very long time. Nothing felt normal. I felt like my pain was a process that would take too long to heal. Trust was a big issue; I felt as though everyone who walked into my life would walk out. I thought, *If my own father had left me, why would anyone else stay?* My mother made the cold hard fact clear for me: my father did not leave based on a change in love or affection; he just needed a rest from his stressful lifestyle. My hole had been filled; I understood that my parents do love me.

Life has thrown many challenges my way. Many people have come into my life, and whether they brought drama, heartbreak, or happiness, my mother has been the one who has stuck through all the heartaches, always wiping my tears like she had done so many times before. My mother is a blessing. She is the one I turn to with all my joys and my problems. She is, and will always be, my best friend.

Yesenia Martinez

I WOULD LIKE TO MEET HIM

At some point in your life, you want to know who that other person is who brought you into the world and how he is or just what he looks like. But at the same time, there's that hatred you have for him and for all the pain he's caused you—all those years that he was not there by your side, when you felt there was no one, no father out there to protect you. That is what is missing in my life.

It was hard for my mom, but our family supported her and helped her get by. I think it would have been better for her if my dad had been there. I didn't think about my dad when I was younger. I had this hate towards him all the time. I thought about it and it made me cry. I never shared my feelings and thoughts about my dad with anyone. So far, I still haven't shared them.

I can't say growing up without a father is hard because I don't have any other experience. I've lived without a dad my whole life. I just cry. Seeing the little girls with their dads at the park or out in the streets gets to me. I can feel the love they have towards their daughters. I wish I had that in my childhood. I didn't think this way before. It never crossed my mind to want a dad.

Once I got older my mind started changing. I wanted to know about my dad, to see what he looks like. I started wondering how things would be if he was here, even if he didn't live with us—just to have someone to stick up for me and then be able to say, "That's my dad"—those small things that don't seem to matter. I wanted to be able to talk to him about boys, given that he was once a teenage boy.

I have an image of how I think my dad would be. We would have lots of things in common. He would be like one of my best friends. We would share the same interests and the same music, and have our own inside jokes. Given that I enjoy

130

music, I couldn't be a day without it. I picture my dad and me just listening to music that we both enjoy and having a good time. I would also like to play the guitar and drums, and have him make my dreams come true, for him to find a school that teaches how to play instruments. I want to try out for soccer and have him help me practice and show me some tricks so I could get better and make the team.

Maybe there are reasons why he left. The one thing that I don't get is why. My mom told me that his dad did the same thing to him, and he hated him for that. So why do it to your own child? Maybe there's something that I just can't understand. Am I too young to understand? If you were not ready to have a kid, why do it in the first place?

I do not like to think that things happen for a reason or that God made it this way. But at times I wonder. I think about how different my life would be if my dad had stayed. I know I wouldn't be where I am right now. I am really close to my family. Family is very important to me. We have our family days, which I love and cherish. I think about how maybe I wouldn't be as close to my family. My grandma probably wouldn't live with us. My whole family helps my mom with my brother and me. They have been with us from day one. I like to look at it as if I have more than one mom and more than just a dad. I have gotten to an age, I guess, where the whole dad thing is really getting to me. But, overall, I wouldn't really want him to be in my life. I just want to know the answers to my questions.

David Camacho

BONDS OF LOVE

The relationship between my dad and his father changed when my dad moved from Mexico to Los Angeles. When my dad was in Mexico, he had a bad job. He washed cars. He got tired of his job because he made very little money. He did not want to tell his parents he was leaving Mexico. When he was halfway to LA, he decided to call his parents and tell them where he was going. When they heard the news, they felt bad. His dad felt especially sad because they had a good relationship.

My dad and grandpa had many laughs. One time my dad told my grandpa this joke about my uncle. He said that my uncle had a really big head. He said he did not look up at the planes because his head was too big and he might have flipped over.

My grandpa also felt sad that my dad moved away because he had been teaching my dad how to play baseball and soccer since my dad was five. My dad started getting good at both sports, so my grandpa decided to start his own baseball and soccer teams and made my dad captain of both.

Every time my dad misses his parents, he sends for them. When my grandpa and grandma come to LA, my dad and grandpa start telling stories—like the time they started their baseball and their soccer teams. When they are here, we go to the park and play baseball. When we are not playing baseball, we are watching the little kids playing baseball. When our favorite soccer team is playing here, we buy tickets to watch the game. We also watch television and play pool. When we are just at home, we tell stories to each other. This is what keeps the relationship between my dad and my grandpa special.

Joshua Cruz

MY FUNNY GREAT GRANDMA

My great grandmother passed away on December 9, 2005. I really cared for her a lot. Because of all the memories I have, I would like other people to know her too. She was a very funny lady.

When she died, my relatives found that she had a lot of money. She lived in a house in El Salvador that her five children helped her build. My relatives found a bag of money and jewelry in her pillowcase. I heard a rumor that someone had found another sack of money and stolen it. My great grandmother saved all the money her children sent over the years, and she was really frugal.

She loved coming to visit us here in America, even though she thought everything here was expensive. Spending fifty dollars on shoes seemed like too much money to her because in El Salvador, a pair of shoes only cost a dollar. I would try to explain to her that in LA, people spend up to one hundred for a pair of Jordans. Her favorite thing to do was to go bargain hunting downtown and to buy material for making her own skirts. She would make clothes and sell them back in El Salvador. One time, she was so proud of bringing home two huge suitcases filled with more than a hundred pieces of clothing.

But she was funny, too; one time, she made me laugh while she was eating rice in our kitchen. It was too hot, but she was too shy to say anything so she ate it anyway. The rice burned her mouth, but she didn't want to go to the hospital. She didn't want to tell my aunt what happened to her. Finally she told my other aunt and they all started to laugh. From then on, she never wanted to eat rice again.

She would always compare everything to El Salvador. When we would go to a Salvadoran restaurant for soup, she would always complain about how much better it tastes in El Salvador. I guess part of what seems so funny now were really just differences between Salvadoran and American culture.

We always loved when she would visit us. Our family treated her with respect, and we were sad to see her pass away. Her other grandchildren were not as friendly or nice to her. They made fun of her and wouldn't even touch the things that she put her hands on. She loved visiting us because we treated her well, and I'm so glad we had such a great relationship.

When I remember my great grandmother and how funny she was, I realize that she distracted me from the hard realities of my life. My relationship with my aunt is serious and stern, but when my great grandma would come to visit, I was always laughing at the funny things she did. I forgot about the things that would normally make me sad, mad, or worried. After a while, I would start to believe that life was pretty good.

Lolbeh Ek

I STILL DON'T KNOW HOW I FEEL

The phone rang around seven in the evening. It was my aunt. She was rambling uncontrollably. My dad ran out the door without saying a word. He had a long, worried look on his face. I had never seen a face like that before. For a second, I ignored it, but it was just too unusual.

My mother was in the shower: she had no idea what was going on. My brother and I couldn't help but stay home waiting for news. We were not sure what was going on. Suddenly, my aunt rushed into our house with her face full of tears. We asked her what was going on. Just as she was going to tell us, my mom came in. My aunt told us all that my uncle Jose was knocked unconscious in front of his house. We freaked out and started to cry.

All my uncles rushed to his house, and the rest of us just waited for the ambulance to arrive. It long and it was awful. We were more relaxed when we heard the ambulance come. Our parents told us that everything was going to be fine. We believed them.

The next day, my family went to the hospital. I walked closely next to my dad. We reached a stop and got inside an elevator. I never really liked elevators, especially in the hospital. When we got out, I remember a long hallway and lots of rooms. My dad and I walked towards one of them. When we entered, I saw my uncle Jose lying in a bed with a machine keeping him alive. It's an image that I still see when I think back. Before all of this, my uncle Jose was a happy person with a lot of ambition. He was always smiling. Immediately, I realized that this was worse than I thought. I went from thinking everything would be fine to wondering what was going to happen. The parents kicked the kids out. We had no choice but to sit outside the room. While we waited, we didn't speak or smile, or do anything, for that matter. I thought back to when Uncle Jose would wake us up early on the weekends just to get chips, ice cream, and candy. I also remembered when he used to stop my cousins and me from fighting, by dragging us and tying the tips of our socks together. I remembered when he used to tease my cousins and me by putting his hand in our faces just to bug us. Right then, I asked myself if my Uncle Jose would ever do these things again or if they would just be memories. All of a sudden, I heard screams coming from the room. Without thinking I rushed in; everyone was crying. I knew my uncle Jose had passed away. I immediately dropped to my knees and cried.

That day was the worst day ever. It was a tragic time for my family. We will treasure the memories we have of Uncle Jose forever. My whole family believes he is still part of us, and he is. My family has a tradition of putting food and water out for special occasions like his birthday or the Day of the Dead. We decorate our houses with pictures of him because it brings comfort and appreciation toward him and toward life.

Noyemi Hadjinian

MY FAMILY—ALWAYS THERE, ALWAYS FUN

The most important thing to me is my family. When I'm going through hard times, I feel they are the only ones I can count on. I have a special relationship with each and every one of them, and I respect them for who they each are as people. They all have wonderful and unique qualities that set them apart from each other. The family that I live with consists of my mother, my brother, and me. My father doesn't live with us because my parents divorced six years ago.

My mother's name is Rebeka, and she is a wonderful human being. She is a single parent raising two kids, has a full-time job, and also takes college classes at night. She always tries to do whatever she can to put our needs first. She is extremely hard-working. We have a great relationship. We have our occasional fights, but they never last more than an hour. She is supportive of my dreams and never questions them.

My father Armen is great, too. He has a demanding job, and he does his best at it. He just started his own candle-making business. He has to make a certain number of candles every day to have a good grip on the business. He does anything he can for us, even if it might be tough sometimes. He and I have a lot in common. We like the same foods, and we look alike. We enjoy talking about those two things.

I have only one sibling—my brother, Vahagn. He just turned eleven years old. (Need I say more?) He is smart and good-hearted. His latest obsession is cars, which he can't stop talking about (bad news for me). He also loves learning about science, history, animals, mysteries, and the world in general. He can be a pest sometimes, but, then again, what eleven-year-old kid isn't? I would never ask for another sibling because I love him so much.

I also love my grandparents. They are humble and honest people who have helped raise my brother and me ever since we were young. They have been married for fifty-six years. My grandmother Srpui is amazing. She is intelligent, lovable, and a great cook. I love entering her house and taking in the aromas of her wonderful food. That is where I get my love for food and cooking. I love listening to her stories about when she was a young girl in Greece, where she was born. She loved school and was an intelligent, hardworking girl. Now, she loves taking care of herself and her home, which is easy to see from the first time you step into her house.

My grandfather Harout is a character. He has the best sense of humor of anyone in our family. He can make us laugh anytime. Even though he is strict, his intentions are good. He helps my mother by taking my brother and me to school and picking us up afterwards.

I have two aunts. My older aunt Anna and I have a lot in common. She and I both love fashion, and our tastes are similar. I love our trips to Beverly Hills and the finest restaurants and shops. She is smart and beautiful and always looks camera-ready.

My younger aunt Maria is fun to be around because we both like to laugh and eat. She is hilarious, and she is the only person I can watch a movie with because my mother and my other aunt tend to always fall asleep in the theater. She has two kids who are my cousins.

My older cousin Emily is close to my age, and we hang out almost every weekend. We are best friends because we think alike, have similar dreams, and understand each other.

My younger cousin Sophie is adorable, feisty, and brave. Spending time with her is entertaining, to say the least. She has a mind of her own, and she can be as stubborn as a mule. You usually don't want to get on her bad side.

I have a lot more family than I have mentioned, and they are all great, but these are the ones to whom I am closest. Most of them live here, and some live in Armenia. Some I know better than others, but one thing is for sure: I love them all equally.

Families are important. They are people who are there for each other. Even if you don't feel that way, your family still plays a big part in your life, and they shape you in some way. Part of being a family is loving one another no matter what, and realizing they are a part of you. You have to learn to accept each other and be grateful for the family that you have. I know I am. I don't know what I would do without them. They are my support system for life.

Paul Zmrutyan

MY CRAZY COUSINS

The two people who have influenced me most are my cousins Artur and Gevo. They were born in Armenia but came to America about five years ago. Artur is twenty-three years old, and Gevo is twenty-five. They are important to me because I can talk about anything I want with them. They talk to me and my cousins Hovo and Harut about sports, cars, girls, mafia movies—just regular guy stuff. But what means the most to me is when they tell me never to fight, because I can see what kinds of fights they went through in the streets of Armenia. One time, when we were in Big Bear, they asked if I had ever fought, and I told them that I had once in self-defense with a Hispanic student. My cousins got a little mad at me, but they had been bad kids in their day, so they understood.

In Armenia my cousins had been in many fights and always got hurt. They fought with rocks and other objects, and small fights led to larger fights, and they were often hurt badly. When they went into the army they did not fight the enemy, but with a soldier in their own unit. The guy pulled a knife on both of my cousins and stabbed them. A different time, they were shot by the same man. Artur was shot in the arm, and Gevo was shot in the leg. This all happened because my cousins were really hyper and got mad too easily. After being shot and stabbed, they both went to the hospital for two weeks. They still have those bullets in their bodies. If the bullets are removed a foot or leg might be paralyzed, because the bullets went through large arteries.

After almost losing their lives, my cousins realized that it wasn't worth it to fight anymore. Their mom and dad always worried about whether or not they would come back alive. After the army my cousins shaped up and went into construction.

Most of the Armenian people who were born in Armenia have never inter-acted with other races; all of their lives they have lived within their own culture. Native Armenians have pride in their own race, and most of the time they don't want to become friends with people from other races. All of this fighting starts because some Hispanics think we're ignorant people. If Armenians and Hispanics would hang out with each other, there would be no fighting. My cousins always said that a small fight would lead up to a bigger fight and possibly even killing, so the right thing to do is not to fight at all. My cousins are like parents to me.

Lusine Muradyan

DOG RUN

When you are a seven-year-old kid playing outside, you do not think anything can happen to you. You feel that because you are a kid, there is no harm coming your way. That was what my mother and I were thinking back in 1997. We thought our neighborhood was safe, and there was nothing that could hurt me or any of the other kids I was playing with. Until that one day.

One sunny afternoon, I decided to go out and play with a couple of friends, as I usually did. We started playing regular games: dodgeball, handball, basketball, etc. It felt liberating. All of us were having so much fun.

As we were playing and yelling, we did not notice a stray dog with pointy ears, sharp teeth, and drool all over him had started to watch us. In the past, my mother would always warn me not to run if I saw a dog, because it would think I was playing with it. Like the time when my neighbor, Gary, was throwing a stick for a dog to catch: Gary ran after the stick instead of the dog, the dog thought Gary was playing with him, and so he ran after Gary and bit him.

Since I didn't know there was a dog there, I ran really fast, screaming and yelling. My team won so we were cheering. At that moment, I noticed the dog looking straight at me. Of course, the dog thought I was running, and he wanted to catch me, so he started running really fast after me. His mouth was open, and his tongue was hanging out with slobber everywhere. I was petrified so I started running even faster, but I could not outrun the dog.

He caught me by my thigh, and would not let me go. I could not feel any pain. I guess that was because I was so terrified. Finally, after thirty seconds of gnawing into my thigh, he let go and ran off. I was in no pain at all and that, to me, was even scarier. I was crying hysterically because I was very scared of what that dog did to my leg. I had never seen such a violent thing in my life, and now it was happening to me.

A minute later, I limped my way home to show my parents my leg. I was afraid that if I walked normally, my foot would fall off. My parents put me in the car and took me to the hospital. I could tell my parents were scared, but they tried really hard not to show it. The blond-haired and blue-eyed doctor who was very tall and skinny took one look at my leg and told my parents I needed seven stitches. At that time, seven stitches seemed like surgery to me. I was so petrified, but my parents were calming me down, telling me that after the stitches they would take me to Chuck E. Cheese's. Surprisingly, that calmed me down, and I felt happier. After the stitches were done, the doctor gave me medicine and a few shots, and told me I was ready to go.

From that day on, I didn't go outside that often, and if I did, it was only with adult supervision. It was not my fear, but that of my mother. The funny thing is that I still love dogs more than anything, and I wish to have one someday. Most people would be scared if a dog bit them, but this incident hasn't changed me at all. I still look at dogs the same way I looked at them before the occurrence.

In the end, I should be thankful I wasn't robbed or killed.

A dog just bit me.

Mariam Keurjikian

SECRET INTELLIGENT SPIES

I remember being a kid and growing up in LA. The world seemed so beautiful and simple. Our parents were always there for us.

My sisters and brother and I grew up in a Christian household where we had to pray before meals. Living in this type of household wasn't easy. If we broke the rules, it was like stepping on a crystal glass. Our parents didn't let us out of their sight and always made sure we were safe. For example, I always wanted to take dancing lessons, but instead I ended up doing martial arts for eight years. We had to learn how to defend ourselves, which was very important. Since I was the oldest, I was usually the one who got the blame for everything. My younger sisters and brother would get into trouble, and it would be my fault. The oldest takes responsibility. This made me feel like I had to make sure that everyone was going by the rules. It really became annoying.

I remember one time my sisters and I were at our friend's house, and we decided to make up this game. We called it S.I.S., Secret Intelligent Spies. This was our only way to escape from the rules set by our parents. It was our own personal world with our own rules. We would make up missions, spy on our family members, and study their personalities. We would draw and make notes about them. We also had our own little exercises that we did before starting each mission. We would do push-ups, sit-ups, jumping jacks, and stretches, and we ran laps around the backyard. Every day held something new and exciting.

I remember one day as if it was last week. It was Father's Day. My sisters and I were at our friend's house playing S.I.S. We were bored, so we decided to explore somewhere new. We ended up going to the house next door. No one lived there. We were outside, looking through the window, and there was nothing but silence. Since we were all young, we were curious to see what was in there. I was eight years old, and everyone else was younger than me. One of my sisters really wanted to open the window and get inside to check out the place. The house was pretty old and looked like it was falling apart. My sister was leaning on the window with her strong arms, trying to get a better look inside. The window couldn't take the pressure and broke. Her arms fell into it.

We all started to freak out because the first thing we saw was a broken window. While we were walking away from the mess, I noticed blood on my yellow shirt. I looked at my sister and couldn't believe what I saw. Both of her arms had ripped, and a big slice of her upper right arm was hanging off. I let out a loud shriek. I was surprised she hadn't noticed or felt any pain whatsoever. It was very hot, and that had probably something to do with it. When she noticed what had happened, we all started panicking and ran home next door. Our screams were probably heard a mile away.

You should have seen the look on our mother's face when we came home. Her big brown eyes were wide open, and her hand covered her mouth. She ran into the kitchen and got the keys to the Benz and a pile of paper towels. They went to the hospital to stitch up my sister's arms.

Since it was Father's Day, our dad's friends had taken him out for a relaxing day off. Little did he know what had happened at home until he received the call and went to the hospital. My sister returned with twenty-four stitches in her right arm and seven stitches in her left. We were so fortunate that she was OK. That was the last time we ever played S.I.S. It's sad that it had to end that way, but it doesn't matter anymore.

I thought I was going to be blamed for everything that had happened and was surprised when my parents didn't get mad at all. I thought there must be something wrong with them, but later on I understood that they were just happy we were alright and knew getting mad wasn't going to help. I'm not sure what was really going through our minds. I guess since we were kids, we were curious about what's really out there. I mean, we were always told what to do and what not to do. Curiosity got the best of us.

My parents were always there for us whenever we needed them. The world is still beautiful but now, I realize, a little more complex.

Jennifer Recio

PINS AND NEEDLES

About a year back, my brother Jorge went to get a checkup because he had a big bump above the back of his knee. The doctors told him it was a tumor. For two weeks, the doctors ran tests to see if the tumor was cancerous. We were all terrified of the results.

The tumor was not cancerous. After a few months, though, Jorge decided he wanted to get it removed because it was bugging him during physical activity. He told my mom he wanted surgery, but she wasn't OK with it—none of us were. We were all very scared. But we wanted him to feel better. My mom, dad, sister, brother, and I talked about this, and we decided to wait.

At a doctor's appointment three months later, Jorge told his doctor he wanted surgery. He didn't tell us until after the appointment. We told him not to get the surgery, but the decision had been made. The doctors told him all the risks: it would be complicated because the tumor grew out of his bone. They were going to cut all the way to the bone, and they would have to move his nerves to get there.

December 21, 2006, was the most nerve-wracking day of my life. My parents and brother woke up at 5:30 a.m. to go to the hospital. I woke up around 8:00 a.m. and called my mom; she gave me the number of the hospital so I could call to get information. Then, I called the hospital, and they told me Jorge wasn't in surgery yet. I called again at 9:00 a.m., and they told me he was going to go into surgery in about half an hour. I called at 11:00 a.m., and they said he was still in surgery. I called every half hour for the next three hours—I think they got tired of me, but it made me laugh. Because I was so nervous, I didn't realize I was calling so much.

Around 3:00 p.m., my mom called me and told me that Jorge was out of surgery and that he was OK. We were relieved he was fine. Later, around 5:30 p.m., he got home, and everyone was happy.

Now that he was home, we were all his nurses. He was on crutches and was not able to keep his leg down too long because blood clots could form and cause complications. We didn't want that, so we all made sure he followed the doctor's instructions. We got him everything he wanted. He would ask for food, ice cream, and the remote—even though he could reach—he was too lazy. He would just tell us to get it. This went on for about two weeks, until he was better.

We are very happy he got his surgery, because now he is more comfortable. He just had a doctor's appointment a week ago, and that doctor told him everything is going well. His cut is almost done scarring.

Daniel Palacios

2007

The 365 days before 2007 did not go so well. They were a complete disaster: each day devastating and unwanted, giving me a feeling of regret. I knew that I was not living life the way I would like. I was desperate and couldn't continue living within a routine that was pulling me down and dragging me out of my comfort zone. I figured the beginning of this year was the only time to leave my old self behind and transform into something better.

When an opportunity to change comes, I take it but somehow end up not doing what I had originally planned. When a new semester begins in school, I say to myself, "This time I'm doing my homework, behaving properly, and working my butt off." Then a couple of weeks pass, I become overwhelmed with assignments, and I decide not to do them at all. I spend precious class time occupied in conversations with fellow students, not always discreetly. This makes my teachers frustrated, which makes me frustrated because they start screaming at me. In reality I frustrate myself, and I'm just not up for that anymore. No, I will work hard and remember every time I write the date on a sheet of paper that my goal is to change for the best this year. I must continue to try to get the best education possible and not surrender to a slothful lifestyle.

My social life in 2006 was not so good, either. Deep down inside I am truly an engaging, mellow guy. Honestly. But people think what they want about me. I am not changing because of others. Being cool with the whole world is never going to happen. I have to remember that the most important factor to this radical transformation is maturity. I hope I can reach a level where I feel comfortable and my friends will still like me. If not, reaching this level is something so special

I am willing to risk losing my friends, even though they are partially the reason I am doing this.

It's finally time to say good-bye to the past year and anxiously welcome in the next. Hopefully I will accomplish every goal set before me. My junior year approaches, and I will try my hardest to do well. I have new people to meet and more friends to make, all thanks to this new year: 2007.

Arlene Rodriguez

THE LAST TWO PIECES TO A PUZZLE

When I was seven or eight years old, my parents separated. I'm using the word "separated" because all I know is they're not together anymore. I don't know if they're still married because we never talk about it. They never talked about what was going on, or how things were going to work out—I just figured things out along the way.

I remember my mom and me packing because we were moving. We didn't take everything, but I was expecting my dad to move in with us. All our clothes were packed, but my dad's weren't (and that should have been a big hint). The bed and the dresser were left behind, but I thought we were just going to go back and get them later.

One night, in the new house, I asked my mom when my dad was going to come. She replied, "He's not." When I asked her why, she just said, "You know why." The problem was I didn't know why. It was like one of those things in the back of your mind you know is there, but never forms into a complete idea. Although I'd rarely seen or heard them fighting, I'd never seen them being affectionate toward each other either. This led me to believe things weren't perfect, and I had an idea they might divorce, but I wouldn't think about it much because I didn't want it to happen. I guess they didn't know what to say to me, or how to say it, so they never said anything. However, I would have preferred an awkward conversation with them rather than being quietly confused.

For a few months after we moved, I didn't see my dad often, which was strange because I was used to spending so much time with him. I would see him only when he would come pick me up from school on his lunch break. Since we were not spending much quality time together, my parents came up with an arrangement for me to spend Tuesdays, Thursdays, and every other weekend with my dad. It felt weird spending the night at our old house for the first time without my mom. I hadn't been there in a while, and I felt like a stranger. The last time I was in that house, we were still a family, but everything had changed since. Walking in didn't feel the same. Now it was my dad's house.

All my things were at my mom's house, so I had to pack clothes just to stay the weekend. Going back and forth only made things more difficult because my parents lived so far from each other. My uncle and aunt had also moved in, and their new baby was now in my room. I was so upset because the baby wasn't even sleeping in there. He would sleep in the crib in my uncle and aunt's room. Staying in my old room would have made me feel more comfortable, but my aunt said that since I wasn't going to be there often, I didn't need the room.

My parents being separated didn't seem to affect me as much when I was younger as it does now that I'm sixteen. As a kid, you just kind of go along with things, and you're happy as long as you get sprinkles on your ice cream. But things are more complicated now. I know both my parents are dating, and it bothers me a lot. I know it's selfish to want them not to date, but it's extremely difficult to accept there's going to be someone else in their lives. I don't know if things will ever get easier, but at least I have both parents, and they try to get along. I think that's what frustrates me—it's like having the last two pieces to a puzzle, but for some reason they won't fit and I don't know why.

Abigail González

THE GRIEF

The death of a loved one is a moment in which all feelings come into one. Some call it grief, defined in the dictionary as a feeling of sadness. This is not even close to what I'd call it. To me grief is a feeling of anger and melancholy. Losing someone and knowing that I am not able to do anything about it because I am only human is a feeling of impotency. I'm often irritated by the way people view life. It's sad and pathetic to see those who don't care.

Life is a precious gift. It goes beyond a religious belief, beyond everything. The heart is the only muscle in the body that can do two things at once: beat and love. It hurts me to see how some are just parasites taking life for granted; they do nothing and live for nothing. There are so many worthless people out there just taking the oxygen and sunlight that other people need, that other people fight to have. Their bodies are worthless shells; they do nothing; they're worth nothing—all they are is trash, and I have to cope with them. I feel sorry for them because they are spiritually dead. Why don't *they* die?

I'm proud to say I know someone whose heart always beat and lived for something: my sister. Her heart beat and lived for me, her big sister. Her heart was the kind of heart that would always try its best, that fought to live, that tried to keep the rhythm no matter how hard it was, even in its last moments. That heart was eight when it gave up. My sister died two years ago this month. You know, sometimes people question how I can talk about it without crying. Here's my answer to that. It hurts. It really does. I like to classify it as a never-ending pain, the pain that sticks to you and follows you even until this very day.

In eleven days my family will gather for the anniversary of her death. I am not nervous or sad; I'm just mad. I'm mad because I miss her. My inner self is burning because everyone's sad, because everyone cries. I hate it. I hate to see my mom cry. Every year it's the same thing; as a matter of fact, it's every day. From morning to night, this feeling is always there.

My family begins preparations in early December. Ever since she passed away, we've always had a memorial. My family, which is pretty big and distinct since I'm mixed with whatever kind of ethnic group you can think of, comes over, and I say a little bit about how everyone in our family is doing. From big to small, we all have the privilege of expressing ourselves and mourning her. The chapel, food, and flowers are all arranged, and so is the limousine that will be carrying us, her family. It's my dad's job to make sure the catering's there on time and to check if they're available. If it's hard for me and I'm just writing, I can't imagine how it is for him. My dad is the strongest guy I know. I don't say this because he's my dad, but because he holds his feelings in when his daughter's dead. I don't judge him, though, because it's not his fault. He was taught to think like a man: a man *never* cries. It's machismo but that's just the way his dad is. My mom is the one in charge of arranging everything that same day: our dresses and the men's tuxedos. The priest, who is too much of a dramatic guy, is her job too. The invitations are my job; I make sure we're not forgetting anyone. It is a long list. We wouldn't like to make anyone feel "left out" (my mom's words). All this seems worthless to me. I mean, give me a break. She's below us, eight feet underground, and she can't see us, so what's the point? I'm sorry if I sound crude—she is my blood after all—but hear me out. It's a very painful process and I'm tired of it.

I'd like to give thanks to my dad for making me like him. I can't cry, Dad. Thank you for raising me with your stupid pathetic way of thinking. You don't know how much I appreciate it. I didn't cry when she died or when I buried her. I just stood there, watching how the dirt slowly covered the place where she was to stay. I didn't cry at all, not because I didn't want to, but because my eyes were dry; they were incapable of having a tear fall from them. I am not a "sentimental" girl, you see. I wasn't raised that way. Crying is a sign of "weakness." I am not weak. I don't like people labeling me as "weak." I cry now because it hurts. It always hurt, but never like today. I finally realized she's "dead," as in not ever coming back. I can't hug her or touch her, much less kiss her.

I hurt because she's gone, because of the impotency I feel. Because I don't hear that little voice that used to whisper in my ear, "I love you." I live because I breathe, and I breathe because of her, because those three words keep me going. Those three words give me the courage to wake up and live, to make something good out of my life. To be the exception, to distinguish myself from the parasites. Those words make me the Abby you see.

Her death will never be forgotten. I will hurt until the day I join her because with her, my life and breath left. It's just another night I sleep alone, another day I spend talking to myself just counting the hours, watching how my life just leaves. Pain is tattooed onto my skin. What do I do with this feeling? She is flesh of my flesh and bone of my bone: she's me. I am trying to heal, and there's nothing I could have done to change the course of things. Life just is and I am only human; I have no power over life. It's up to Him: the higher power, the one I owe my existence to.

I'm trying to heal, so just please let it go. It is a wound starting to build a scab, and it's prepared to scar. Please, because every time we do this it seems to keep on opening, and it bleeds; it bleeds and it doesn't stop. I just want it to heal. I have already learned that between you and the one you love there may be distance, but no one, no power will ever part you. Death is not my boundary; I have no boundaries.

My feelings for her cannot be described. The day she died my stupidity and ignorance died. My perspective towards life changed; everything changed. I am not glad she's gone; it hurts that this had to happen. It happened so I could change; so I could treasure life. It hurt at first; it still hurts, just not as much. Grief is here and no closer to being gone. It gets easier, don't get me wrong. Dad, Mom, she is in everything I see, in all that I am, and I know every time I think of her she's right here in my heart. But I guess until you understand, I will just have to cope with it and with my process of grief.

Rest in peace.

Rest in God.

Melanie Perez

MY BEAUTIFUL LIFE

It was January 11, 2003, in Guatemala City. I was thinking how beautiful the flowers in my garden were. I was eleven years old, the sky was blue, the sun was shining, and the birds flew peacefully. I was going up the stairs as my father passed me. He seemed to be in a hurry. My father answered the phone. He said, "Yes. Hello, hello, it's me, Eddie. Oh, no…"

When he hung up, he immediately called to my mother. I knew it was bad news, so I stayed quiet. I heard my father say, "They killed him. They did. And all I know is that I am next. We have to go to your brother in California."

My mother panicked and said, "Fine, we'll go. Don't tell the kids. I'll tell them we're going on one of our vacations to California."

"It's fine," said my father.

As my mother murmured, the phone rang again. It was my grandpa telling my father that he had gotten the last five tickets for the five o'clock plane. My father said that was great and told my grandpa that we were going to be away for six months. I didn't panic, but I was nervous because I didn't know who "they" killed or why we were going to be away for six months. All I could think about was what my father said: "All I know is that I am next."

Immediately I thought of four years earlier. Two men killed my uncle, and my daddy said then, "All I know is that I could be next." After the death of my uncle, we went to California for six months. My mom was pregnant and gave birth during our third month there. We came back and everything was fine until my grandfather became the head of the police force for all of Guatemala. He became powerful and started to receive death threats. My mother called them "rare notes." I could only

154

imagine what they said.

My two brothers and I were very excited about going back to California. We packed everything we thought we needed. My oldest brother Armando said, "Oh, California, it means Disneyland, Six Flags, Big Bear, and many other places. Right, Mommy?"

"Yes," she answered. "Now hurry, and try not to disturb your father. Take everything downstairs, and put it in your uncle's car. He will take us to the airport. But listen, there will be two more cars, one in front and one in the back following us at all times. Act like you don't know."

Nobody asked questions. My two brothers and I acted like we had no mouths. Even though I knew what was happening, I pretended that I didn't know. I thought my oldest brother knew what was going on, but I was scared to ask him. We were all afraid to say anything so we were silent—all the way to Los Angeles.

My uncle was waiting for us at the airport. It was the first time I had seen him in four years. We were all very excited, but tired, so we fell asleep as soon as we got to his house. The next day the phone woke me up. It was my grandpa saying that "they" killed my daddy's best friend. We all panicked because it was a bloody killing. They had shot him twenty times and then killed his bodyguard, thinking it was my dad.

A month passed. Then two, then three, until the sixth month, when I heard my parents arguing about what was going to happen. They said that we couldn't go back. Everything was still too dangerous; Grandpa was still getting threat letters. One day my uncle came and said he had good news. He told me I had been accepted to my cousin's middle school. I didn't like the idea. It meant we were going to stay even longer.

When I started school, I cried every day. I had no friends. Everyone spoke a different language and was a different ethnicity than I was. I studied English and understood every single word the teachers said, but the problem was that I am a very shy person and felt embarrassed to read or talk in front of the other kids.

I hated this country. I hated where I lived. It was so different from Guatemala. In Guatemala, I lived in a very big house with my own room. I never thought or worried about not having what I wanted. I never appreciated what I had. After coming to this country, I saw my life differently. Now, if I get a pair of shoes, I take good care of them and the old pair. I won't rip them and throw them away. I will look for a poor girl who needs a pair of shoes. I also learned how to appreciate my parents. And now, I thank this country for letting my family stay here. Otherwise I wouldn't have my dad here next to me, holding me, loving me, and even screaming at me. He would be in heaven.

Four years after leaving Guatemala, I had enough confidence to ask my parents the truth. Respectfully, I told my mother to sit on one side of the table and my father on the other side; my mother's eyes were already welling up with tears. I couldn't stop crying either. "OK," my mother said. "Well, you know how everything started. Two men killed your daddy's friend while your dad was in the car behind." My mother paused. "Honey, I'm so sorry that at your young age you had to live through this."

Before my mother finished the rest of the story, I started talking and told my parents all the things I had in my head, things I had thought of telling them before. I said, "Mom, Dad, I really thank God for giving me parents like you. I wouldn't trade you with any other kid for billions of dollars. I am so sorry that for the last three years I was a rebel. I really wanted to go back to Guatemala. I never told my friends where I was. I can't imagine how worried they were. But you need to know that this did not ruin my life. Instead it gave me a kick and woke me up from the dream that I was living in Guatemala. It was a life of fun, friends, and money, but I didn't even see you, Dad. You were always at your office. Or Mom, you were with your friends having tea. Now you're at home. Dad, we get to talk. Mom, we get to play. I want you to know how much I love you, how important you are to me. I can't imagine living without you, Dad. I wouldn't want to go back to the way things were in Guatemala if it meant losing you. Parents always want the best for their kids and you've given me the best thing: love. Well, I guess I just want to thank you for being my parents."

I asked my mom to stop telling me the story. I had heard enough. It was too painful to think about it anymore. I am a new person now who hopes to go back to her country someday to visit her friends and family. I am just an average girl who goes to school. I am not going to lie: sometimes at night, I still cry because it hurts that my grandma calls every Tuesday and Thursday because she misses us. I ask God, "Why did this have to happen to me if there are millions of girls out there?" Nobody has the answer. But I know that if I am good and I study, I will one day give my parents back all that they gave me. This story ends with a happy family, now safe in a warm house.

ACKNOWLEDGMENTS

The Elotes Man Will Soon Be Gone would not be possible without the effort and resolve of so many—Jane Patterson's students in the Humanitas program at John Marshall High School, the Marshall faculty and staff, and dozens of volunteers at 826LA. First and foremost, we recognize the students for their hard work. They wrote for a solid month and followed that with repeated editorial meetings, some of which took place while school was not in session. The result is the book you hold in your hands.

We at 826LA must thank those at Marshall who helped lead this project. Without Jane Patterson's support and dedication, we would not have been able to coordinate tutoring times or schedule editorial board meetings. More importantly, her vision and guidance laid the foundation for this anthology: she crafted the assignment that led to the writing of these essays and shepherded her students through their first drafts. We also recognize the rest of the tenth-grade Humanitas team—David Dandridge, Teri Klass, and Paul Payne—as well as assistant principal Bob DiPietro and new principal Daniel Harrison for their support of this collaboration between Humanitas and 826LA. Likewise, we thank assistant principal Jerry Devries; B-track counselors George Ono, Martha Garate, and Sabrina Gedemer; Jose Rodriguez; Jorge Espinoza; the John Marshall School Site Council; and the Urban Education Partnership for supporting the Humanitas program that has now partnered with 826LA to produce two books.

Of course, this book could not have happened without the aid of 826LA's volunteers. Some worked side by side with students on draft after draft; others edited dozens of student essays. We acknowledge them all here.

These tutors helped guide the students' writing in the classroom: Adam Baer, Steve Basilone, Emily Benz, Julie Carpineto, Jade Chang, Diane Clemenhagen, Erin Foster, Marcy Freedman, Herb Jordan, Meghan Kelley, Tracy Mazuer, Michelle Mizner, Jessie Nagel, Joshua Peralta, Heidi Pickman, Mana Pirnia, Pamela Ribon, Alex Riguero, and Kellie Schmitt.

And the following volunteers spent hours editing the student work: Melissa Crowley, Cori Doherty, Beth Goodhue, Nancy Hanna, Laura Hertzfeld, Liz Miller, Justin La Mort, Tracy Mazuer, Jill K. Murphy, Heidi Pickman, Kellie Schmitt, Ann Shen, Jacob Strunk, Marie Claire Tran, Judy Tsuei, Sobrina Tung, Diane Wright, and Ian A. Young.

826LA's interns, too, must be recognized for all that they do—typesetting, proofreading, translation, meeting with students, and providing general publication support. Over the course of this project, the following interns helped: Kelly Broffman, Jessica Burkhart, Bonnie Chau, Julia Deixler, Esther Hamm, Loretta McCormick, and Rory Vallis.

The student editorial board deserves special recognition for all that they have done. In addition to writing and polishing their own essays, they stayed for hours after school, week after week, whether school was in session or not, to conceptualize the finished book and write the introduction. Neither their teachers nor the 826LA staff hesitated to entrust them with important decisions or more responsibility. They are Rebecca Bowden, Margareth Lobo, and Melanie Perez, and it has been our pleasure to work with such intelligent, mature young minds.

We must thank Jill K. Murphy again, this time for her exceptional work with the student editorial board. We are also especially grateful to Heidi Pickman for masterminding and coordinating the radio production of some of this book's essays, as well as Travis Schooley for his brilliant book design. Lastly, we give our warmest thanks to Teresa Burkett Bourgoise, who brought Marshall High School and 826LA together, thus catalyzing this amazing project.

Thanks, once again, to all involved: the volunteers and donors who've made this book and all other 826LA programming possible. And thanks to the noble, benevolent *elotero*, the central symbol for this book, a symbol for our city and our time.

—Mac Barnett, Amy Orringer, Danny Hom, and Julius Diaz Panoriñgan

ABOUT 826LA

826LA helps students, ages 6 to 18, with their writing skills, whether in the realm of creative writing, expository writing, or English-language learning. We offer free drop-in tutoring, after-school classes, storytelling events, and assistance with student publications.

TUTORING IS AT THE HEART OF IT

Our method is simple: we assign free tutors to students so that the students can get one-on-one help. It is our belief that great advancement in English skills and comprehension can be made within hours if students are given concentrated help from knowledgeable tutor-mentors.

FIELD TRIPS

We want to help our teachers get their students excited about writing while also helping students to be better at expressing their ideas. We welcome teachers and their classes for field trips during the school day. A group of tutors is on hand at every field trip, whether we are helping to generate new material or revise already-written work. Our most popular field trip is Storytelling & Bookmaking; the entire class works together with our tutors to create a story, along with illustrations, and each student leaves with his/her own book.

WORKSHOPS

Our tutors are experts in all different areas of writing, from comic books to screenplays to science fiction. That's why we're able to offer a wide variety of free workshops to studens. One of our favorites so far, "ImagiNation: If I Were King or Queen…" allows students the opportunity to create their own country, replete with maps, flags, and laws.

IN-SCHOOL PROJECTS

The strength of our volunteer base allows us to make partnerships with Los Angeles-area schools. We coordinate with teachers and go en masse to schools and work with students in their classrooms. For example, if a history teacher at Venice High feels her students could use extra help revising a paper on violence in the Middle East, she could ask 826LA for support from five tutors for her 2:00 p.m. Thursday class. Tutors will arrive, ready to work one on one.

For more information,
please visit 826LA.org
or email info@826LA.org.